MVFOL

"Who *are* you?" Moira asked, hands on her hips. "More important—where am I?"

"Sit, child of man . . . and woman . . . and I will reveal all." The fox's shoulders moved up and down. He seemed to be chuckling.

Moira sat. In such a short time, she'd learned a kind of obedience. The stone floor was not as cold as she'd feared.

The fox sat, too, and curled his bushy tail around his feet. "You are in Trollholm. And that creature who captured your friends was Aenmarr the troll, whose bridge you came over at sunset."

"A troll? You have *got* to be kidding!" Moira wondered if the whole thing was some sort of dream. Had she fallen asleep while driving? "You mean like trit-trot, trit-trot . . . the three billy goats going over a bridge and . . ."

"This is no fairy story," the fox said, his pink tongue suddenly slipping out between his teeth.

Remembering the troll's awful protruding teeth and the photographer ground between them, Moira shivered. "No happily ever after?" she asked.

"Not for everyone," the fox told her. "Perhaps not for anyone."

trollbridge

A ROCK 'N' ROLL FAIRY TALE

JANE YOLEN AND ADAM STEMPLE

A TOM DOHERTY ASSOCIATES BOOK
NEW YORK

This is a work of fiction. All the characters, organizations, and events portrayed in this novel are either products of the authors' imagination or are used fictitiously.

TROLL BRIDGE: A ROCK 'N' ROLL FAIRY TALE

A Starscape Book
Published by Tom Doherty Associates, LLC
175 Fifth Avenue
New York, NY 10010

www.tor.com

ISBN-13: 978-0-7653-5284-2
ISBN-10: 0-7653-5284-2

First Edition: July 2006
First Mass Market Edition: July 2007

Printed in the United States of America

0 9 8 7 6 5 4 3 2 1

～

"Prince Charming Comes" was first printed as a poem in *Storyteller*, a collection by Jane Yolen (NESFA Press, 1992) and recorded as a song © 1995 by The Flash Girls on *Maurice and I* (Fabulous Records).

∾ Contents ∾

∾ From the Authors ∾

We have relied on two famous fairy tales for this book, "The Three Billy Goats Gruff " and "The Twelve Dancing Princesses," as well as assorted troll legends.

"The Three Billy Goats Gruff " is a Norwegian story, and the version everyone knows best was collected in 1845 by Peter Christen Asbjornsen and Jorgen Moe, though similar stories have been found in other countries and cultures. Basically a trickster tale, it shows the trolls to be large, mean, and stupid. Or at least pretty slow.

Trolls (especially as we show them here) are of Scandinavian extraction. So what better place to set them down than in the American Midwest, where many Swedes and Norwegians settled in the middle and later years of the nineteenth century. As Adam lives in Minneapolis, he is able to speak firsthand of the cultural heritage there. This includes the real Dairy Princesses, whose heads are sculpted in butter, a Minnesota tradition. However, if you have a map handy, do not waste your time looking for Vanderby. While Minneapolis, the Twin Cities, and Duluth are all real places, we made up Vanderby, its river, and the stone bridge. The name Vanderby is a cobbled-together Norwegian word meaning something like *Waterbridge* or *Watergate*.

We started with the "Three Billy Goats Gruff " and then decided to add the Dairy Princesses to the mix for some more excitement. For that bit, we have relied on the Grimm story of "The Twelve Dancing Princesses," a story known under several other names as well, such as "The Worn Shoes" and "The Shoes That Were Danced to Pieces." Sometimes the folk story is about one princess who wears out twelve pairs of shoes but more often, the story is of twelve girls, three nights, and an assortment of doomed princes who try to rescue them. The story probably goes back to the seventeenth century and is most often found in central Europe.

As for the Scandinavian Fossegrim (Foé-say-grim), he is considered a guardian spirit of waterfalls and an expert harper or fiddler who is also—when he feels like it—a master music teacher. It's said he can play music to make graybeards leap up dancing from the hearthside and to bring milk to a maiden's breast. Messy, that. But his teaching comes at a price, for he is a trickster, and his help is unreliable.

1 · Dairy Princess

∾

And he was singing:
What's better than a butter girl?
Badder than my better girl.
Best when I'm not buttered up as well.
What's better than a butter girl?
Badder than my better girl.
Best that I just take them all to Hell.

—Words and music by
Jakob and Erik Griffson,
from *Troll Bridge*

Radio WMSP: 10:00 A.M.

"So, Jim, here it is, another Monday morning, and we have twelve new Dairy Princesses. But I hear this year is a bit different than other years."

"Why yes, Katie, quite a bit different. This year we have the usual crop of star athletes and straight-A students, ready to promote the dairy industry throughout the five-state area. But there's also Moira Darr, a genuine prodigy."

"A prodigy, Jim? How so?"

"She's sixteen and performs with the Minnesota Orchestra. First chair harpist. She's international concert rank, and local composers have been lining up to write pieces for her. Her parents have said she has to finish high school before they'll let her turn professional, though."

"Well, good for them! And what is she like, young Moira Darr?"

"[Laughs.] Pretty, as you'd expect. Long blond hair. Startling blue eyes. But she's also very strong-minded and outspoken."

"Guess she'd have to be, Jim, working alongside adults as she does. Holding her own, don't you know."

"Yep. When I told her she looked and played like an angel, she quoted some famous musician, saying: 'To play like an angel, you have to work like the devil.'"

"That's good. I'll have to remember that. But I hear there's more than just young Ms. Darr that makes this year's Dairy Princesses unique."

"You can say that again. As you know, Katie, every year, the princesses get likenesses of themselves carved in butter that are displayed in the Agriculture Building at the State Fair."

"I saw them, Jim, and a lovely presentation it was, too. Remind us what happens after the State Fair."

"Well, normally, the butter sculptures are driven to Vanderby, a small town near Duluth, where they are left on the Trollholm Bridge."

"Why?"

"No one knows. Or at least no one's telling. Those folks in Vanderby . . . [Laughs.]"

"Now, Jim, I come from near there. [Laughs.]"

"Sorry, no offense meant."

"None taken, Jim. But you were saying . . ."

"Displaying the butter heads at the State Fair has been a tradition since 1965. But residents of Vanderby say that leaving the butter heads at the bridge goes back years before that. Even back to the days when the first Scandinavian immigrants settled in Minnesota."

"They had Dairy Princesses back then?"

"They had sculptures in butter back then, Katie. The Dairy Princesses only go back to the 1930s."

"So the princess butter heads have been going on for, let's see, over seventy years at least. Every year?"

"Every year till this one."

"So this year was different?"

"Very different, Katie. Feign McGuigan, a real estate magnate from the East Coast, felt the nearly one thousand pounds of melting butter on the bridge was a danger to the sportfishing industry. He, and his eight-million-dollar campaign chest, won a seat as mayor of Vanderby, and eliminating the annual butter deposit has been his only executive action to date."

"Out of curiosity, what was his opponent's campaign budget?"

"Twelve hundred dollars. And he said that was stretching it."

"Thanks, Jim. We'll have more on that story as it develops. Now here's Bob with sports."

· 1 ·

Moira

The regular Tuesday rehearsal had taken longer than planned because the trombone section had made a hash of their parts. It was already four thirty and Moira was furious. She banged her fist on the steering wheel. She was supposed to be in Vanderby by seven *and* in her Dairy Princess finery. Yet here she was, not even out of the Twin Cities, fighting traffic, and still in her jeans.

Trombonists are the worst! she thought. Then she spoke her anger aloud: "If I can practice a full solo to perfection while going to high school—carrying a 4.0 average, too— they should be able to get their lives together enough to learn twenty bars properly."

Making a face at one of the drivers who was trying to edge in ahead of her, Moira cursed under her breath. She'd never say any such thing aloud. At sixteen and in an adult profession, she'd learned to use her niceness well. Outspoken—but said sweetly. That was the way to do it. However, this day wasn't going as planned. And Moira preferred things to go the way they were written down in her schedule book.

Easing out onto Route 35W, she slipped a rehearsal tape of her solo into the tape deck, and listened critically as she drove. There was one run that still gave her a bit of trouble, though she doubted anyone—not even the conductor—had noticed. But of course she knew. *And who else counts, after all?*

Suddenly, she remembered she hadn't phoned her parents, so reluctantly, she pulled over onto the grass and stopped the car. Her part of the driving-alone bargain was to stay in touch. *And really,* she thought, *they aren't asking much.*

She turned on the phone, which she'd turned off during rehearsal. Orchestra policy insisted on it. And they were right. Nothing worse than ten different cell phones going off while the musicians were wrestling with a difficult passage. Since it was orchestra policy, her parents couldn't complain.

She glanced at the readout. Yes—three messages, all from her mother. She'd better call before her father got the police involved. *Stage parents can sometimes be the worst,* she thought. Especially her parents.

Her mother picked up on the first ring. Moira started talking before her mother said hello. It was better if she didn't let her mother get a word in.

"Just leaving the city, Mom," she said. "Got a late start. Not my fault. You wouldn't believe how bad the trombones were. We had to go over their stuff eight times. Eight! Really! What a mess. Maestro was not amused." Of course no one called him Maestro except as a joke. "And they wanted to put me behind the strings. *Behind!* I reminded Maestro that my contract called for me to be between the winds and the strings so I can hear. Good contract. Thanks, Mom." She could almost see her mother smiling at that.

"Call when you get to Vanderby," her mother replied, the moment Moira took a breath.

"I will." And she would, too, or there went her driving privileges. "Love you."

Next she called Helena, the chief Dairy Princess, to tell her that she was just leaving the city. Helena made rude noises on the phone in return, adding she'd stall everyone when they got to Vanderby. "But get here before it's dark. And don't dawdle." *Dawdle* was Helena's favorite word.

"I never dawdle," Moira said, meaning it. Then she turned off the phone. There was no time to lose if she was going to make the photo shoot.

She made a face at the thought, though: another photo op. What a waste of good practice time. She'd only tried out for Dairy Princess in the first place because her parents thought the exposure would help her career. The whole thing was supposed to take only a few days of smiling competition, interviews, crowning, a few parades. The event itself had been a bit silly, and a bit sweet. She liked the girls. Well, some of them. Especially Helena, who had a smart mouth. And Kimberleigh, who was a black belt in karate but looked as if she'd never done anything more strenuous than file her nails. The rest of them were pleasant enough, and very serious, or at least serious about being Dairy Princesses. However, not a one of them knew anything about classical music, which was a drag. Their musical tastes ranged from sugary pop to dance, with one—Chantelle—going for rap. Which, in Moira's opinion, was as close to music as ad copy was to poetry.

But a week of being a DP was about as much as she was willing to invest, with her busy schedule. And here, six days after the last of it, the local paper suddenly wanted to do a full spread in their weekend edition about the controversy boiling up around the new Vanderby mayor, a Mr. McGuigan. Which the princesses were somehow part of, though she wasn't sure how. Since the princesses had each signed a contract to do appearances for a full year—though no more than one a month—Moira had been stuck. Besides, the dairy people had been so accommodating, working the shoot around her schedule of rehearsals, she had nothing left to complain about except that she had to do it.

Shut up, Moira! she scolded herself, as she often did.

BY SEVEN FIFTEEN, DRIVING LEAD-FOOTED all the way, Moira was beyond Duluth and heading toward Vanderby and its Trollholm bridge. Her mother's typed instructions had been perfect so far.

"Thanks, Mom," she called out the window, as though her mother could hear her all the way in St. Paul.

Moira was glad she hadn't driven with the other girls anyway. The time alone had given her a good start on listening to a tape of what would be her newest solo, a piece called "Waiting on the Princess," written especially for her by Daniel Berlin, Minnesota's most famous composer, world famous, in fact. He'd never written for harp before, which made the piece very difficult, and it would be a good stretch for her. She was about to play the tape again when a green sign announced the turn for Vanderby.

She pulled off the main road and onto a dirt drive her mother had marked as "Very rural."

"That's an understatement," Moira said aloud, looking at the pine trees that threatened to crowd her off the road. She almost missed the smaller path that her mother had marked in large letters: "DON'T OVERSHOOT."

It was bumpy, so she slowed down to fifteen miles an hour and when that seemed too fast, she downshifted to about eight. Then the trees opened up a bit and there, ahead of her, were several cars and a van parked near a gray stone bridge.

Moira breathed deeply. *Made it!*

Pulling between Helena's blood-red Acura and the newspaper's gray van, she stopped the car and popped the trunk where her princess dress, crown, and shoes were carefully placed. She leaped out, waving at the other girls who'd draped themselves in various positions along the bridge's low stone walls.

The photographer was already set up and taking some early shots of individuals. Behind them the sun was just starting down behind two towering pines.

"I'm here!" Moira shouted. "I made it."

Helena stood, putting her hands on her hips and looking every inch a royal. Her Dairy Princess crown glittered red in the sun's rays. "For goodness sakes, girl, stop dawdling and get dressed in your gear!"

"I'll be quick."

The photographer turned and growled at her, "*Mighty* quick, honey. Before the light goes, please." He moved onto the bridge with the girls, leaning in for close-ups. She could hear him talking rapidly to them, cozening them, getting them to smile. "Like the princesses you are," he said. "Not cheese, caviar."

"Caviar . . ." they replied dutifully, smiling prettily and opening their eyes wide, though Moira doubted any of them had ever actually tasted caviar. She had, at her first symphony gala. The stuff was fishy-tasting and awful.

Moira had just started to turn back toward her car to get into her princess clothes, when she heard an odd, rushing sound, like the timpani in Stravinsky's "Rites of Spring," loud, insistent, pounding. She listened more carefully. No, it sounded more like a train.

But we're nowhere near any train, she thought, looking over her shoulder toward the sound.

And then she saw it, a wall of water rushing down the river, almost as high as the trees. It was heading right toward the bridge—toward the girls and the photographer—traveling with the mindlessness of any natural phenomenon.

Moira spun around and ran toward them. "Get off the bridge," she screamed. "Now!" She pointed to the water galloping their way.

For a moment everything seemed in motion, the girls and the photographer looking up, seeing Moira, hearing her, following her pointing finger. And then, like deer in the headlights, they stopped. None of them moved, not an arm, not a leg, not one step off the Trollholm Bridge.

The roaring water rolled over them—and they were gone.

· 2 ·

Moira

For a long moment Moira couldn't move, either. Only her heart, which was beating frantically, kept going. She stared at the wall of water, blue, white, green, the top waves tipped with red from the rays of the setting sun.

And then—she couldn't quite figure out how—she looked right into the water in front of her, and realized with a gasp that there was a figure inside it.

Impossible! Yet there it was, in the middle of all that rushing water. A huge figure, greenish, human. Well, human-ish, anyway, but big as a house. It was wearing some sort of trousers and a kind of shirt, which hung outside the pants.

Oh God! Moira thought.

For a second Moira closed her eyes, but what she'd already seen was still imprinted on the inside of her lids: the giant man-thing turning away from her, with the eleven girls clutched in its hands and the photographer . . . the photographer was in the creature's mouth, held there between enormous protruding teeth.

"Let them go!" Moira screamed at it. But her cry was obscured by the rush of water and by the screams of the other girls.

It was Moira's own scream that gave her momentum. Her body knew before her brain that she had to save them. If she'd actually given it any thought, she'd never have tried. But she raced to the bridge, leapt one-footed onto the low wall, and then launched herself at the creature's back. She caught the end of its shirttails and hung on.

"You . . . You . . ." She couldn't think of a curse strong enough. "You monster."

Shut up, Moira! she thought. The last thing she needed to do now was alert the monster that she was hanging on to him. *And what, in the name of Bach, Brahms, and Bartok, am I doing dangling dangerously on the back end of a giant creature like some crazed movie hero, way above a rushing river, when I should be back in my car, calling the police on my cell phone?*

She glanced down.

Mistake. *Big* mistake. Way below her, the river not only rushed, it hurtled, churned, tumbled, roared.

Lucky I'm not afraid of heights, she told herself. *But, I think I'm scared spitless of giant monsters.*

And it was too late—way too late—to let go.

THE MONSTER ALIEN CREATURE THING walked for minutes, hours, days. Moira had no idea how long. She simply held on to his shirttails with her strong fingers, fingers that practiced harp three to five hours a day. She clutched the sloppy wet material and prayed.

But after a while, she could feel herself starting to slip down the shirttails, fingers so cold and cramped, she couldn't hold on any longer. Her hands were strong, but not *that* strong.

Don't scream, she warned herself. *Don't make a sound.* But the breath rushed out of her as she fell, screaming. She landed with an awful crunch, not in the river as she had feared, but on stone.

Ouch, she thought. It was the last thought she had for quite some time.

SHE HEARD A VOICE.

"Do not move or Aenmarr will return."

"Aenmarr? What's an Aenmarr?" She was crumpled up on her side with her eyes closed. She was afraid to open them, her head hurt so bad. Any sort of light and her skull might explode.

"Shhhhhh, child of man."

She lay still but muttered, "Child of man and woman actually."

The voice sighed wearily. "If you value your life, be quiet."

Shut up, Moira! she told herself and was quiet, but she groaned inwardly, *What have I gotten myself into?*

"Trouble, human child. Trouble."

It's in my head! The voice was in her head. It knew what she was thinking. Gasping, Moira tried to sit up.

"Shhhh!"

Something warm and soft pressed against her side, holding her down.

Closing her mouth, she let the warm thing push her back down. *Shut up, Moira,* she warned herself again.

"Now you understand."

But she didn't understand, not really. She didn't understand who Aenmarr was, or where it came from, or who the voice was, or what—she thought in a rush—she was doing lying on stone.

Maybe she'd drowned in that wall of water and this was the afterlife. Only it seemed very hard for Heaven and too cool for Hell.

"Not what, but who. When Aenmarr passes, I will tell you all," the voice assured her. "Now, hush."

Oh, she thought, *Aenmarr is the alien monster.*

She put her head back down and waited. Till Aenmarr passed, got in his spaceship, and went back to Mars, or fairyland or wherever. "When Aenmarr passes." It sounded like a title of one of Daniel Berlin's pieces, and she thought—a bit hysterically—*I'll have to tell him.* Though as she thought this, a traitor part of her was afraid she was never going to get to tell anyone anything again.

AFTER A WHILE—A LONG while in which she didn't dare move, even to check her watch—the voice in her head said, "Rise human child. Follow me."

She stood gingerly, felt for broken bones, found none,

though she bet she'd find bruises soon enough. It was now dark, a deep and relentless dark, darker than night should have been, and she wondered briefly how she was going to be able to follow what she couldn't see. She also wondered about finding the girls, wondered how to go about rescuing them. She guessed—she knew—that the photographer was beyond help.

Something slightly lighter than the dark moved ahead of her. She put out a hand to touch it. Felt fur. Heard a growl.

Withdrawing her hand quickly, she whispered, "Sorry," to the creature, the dog, whatever.

"Follow," it said, "but do *not* touch me again."

"Sorry," she repeated, and followed.

AFTER A TIME, SHE REALIZED that though she hadn't actually broken any bones, she ached everywhere. Her fingers were stiff, her back was sore, her arms felt as if they'd been pulled from their sockets and then been replaced badly. Her head was hammering away as if someone were beating out the four opening notes of Beethoven's Fifth on her skull over and over and over again.

The voice in her head told her, "Come straight, now left, step over the rock, now left again."

She might as well have been blind in that deep dark. She stopped and looked around. *Rescue the girls? First I have to rescue myself.*

"How," came the answer, "will you even rescue yourself if you do not listen?"

She who always had an answer, had none.

At last the voice said, "Duck," only she didn't duck fast enough and banged the top of her head on what she later realized was the entrance to a low cave. It set her headache clanging again. She had to drop to her knees and crawl in.

"That wasn't funny," she whispered to the creature ahead of her.

"It was not meant to be."

The cave opening was narrow in the beginning but widened quickly.

"You can stand now if you wish."

Moira stood slowly, her hands above her just in case. Relieved, she stretched to her full height. The cavern was lit with a strange phosphorescent light. As her vision adjusted to it, she began to make out the softly rounded cave walls. Turning, she saw the light reflected in a pair of dark eyes. The creature who'd guided her to the cave was smaller than she expected, and to her surprise was neither alien nor dog, but a fox, male, with two jaunty ears and a long furry tail.

"Who *are* you?" she asked, hands on her hips. "More important—where am I?"

"Sit, child of man . . . and woman . . . and I will reveal all." The fox's shoulders moved up and down. He seemed to be chuckling.

Moira sat. In such a short time, she'd learned a kind of obedience. The stone floor was not as cold as she'd feared.

The fox sat, too, and curled his bushy tail around his feet. "You are in Trollholm. And that creature who captured your friends was Aenmarr the troll, whose bridge you came over at sunset."

"A troll? You have *got* to be kidding!" Moira wondered if the whole thing was some sort of dream. Had she fallen asleep while driving? "You mean like trit-trot, trit-trot . . . the three billy goats going over a bridge and . . ."

"This is no fairy story," the fox said, his pink tongue suddenly slipping out between his teeth.

Remembering the troll's awful protruding teeth and the photographer ground between them, Moira shivered. "No happily ever after?" she asked.

"Not for everyone," the fox told her. "Perhaps not for anyone."

Tears suddenly filled Moira's eyes. She didn't know if she was crying for herself, or for the captured girls, or for the poor photographer she'd last seen in Aenmarr the troll's mouth. But she couldn't stop the tears from coming, and soon sobs racked her body sending fat sloppy tears to splash onto the stone cave floor.

The fox licked its fur and watched her impassively, his eyes like obsidian.

· 3 ·

Moira

Moira hadn't meant to sleep. But the long rehearsal and long drive, and then everything after, all combined to knock her out.

Or else it was magic. She couldn't be sure.

When she awoke, her eyes were crusted as if she'd been sleeping for days with a fever. An oddly muffled booming sounded behind her. *Waterfall?* she wondered. But when she turned to look, she couldn't see a thing.

Turning over on her side, she noticed a half circle of light about a hundred feet away, slowly growing in intensity. Underneath her was stone. It took her a minute to remember where she was.

Only, of course, she didn't believe it. She *couldn't* believe it. It had to be a dream or a nightmare or, she thought, a coma.

That was it. She'd fallen asleep in the car somewhere after

Duluth or even right before turning into Vanderby, and driven off the road. Probably she was now in a hospital. Her mother and dad had certainly been called, because she had a who-to-call card in her wallet and another in her glove compartment. Her mom had insisted on it. So they were probably already in the hospital room, weeping over her, waiting for her to wake up.

"Mom . . ." she whispered. "Dad . . ." She closed her eyes and tears seeped onto her cheeks.

Then she opened them again and looked at the half circle of light once more. She'd read about such a thing. Soon someone from her past, someone dead—maybe her grandmother Darr, or her first harp teacher, Mr. Mikelson—would appear and call to her. And she would go toward the light. She would go—and die.

I don't want to die, she thought. *I'm only sixteen. I only just got my license.*

Suddenly she saw a figure filling the half circle of light and she began to shiver, though not from being cold. The figure was the fox.

"Hungry, human child?" he called out, his voice breathy in her head.

And she was. Though frightened, stunned, numb, freezing, and weepy, she discovered with astonishment, she was also enormously hungry.

"Famished," she said, starting to crawl toward the cave opening.

The fox trotted over to her, opened his mouth, and dropped a dozen or so beetles in front of her. They looked dead, except for one that was still waggling its front feet feebly.

Stomach acid rose up and pooled in Moira's mouth. *I'd rather starve,* she thought.

"If that is your wish," said the fox. He put his head to one side quizzically and stared at her till she was forced to look down. The almost-dead beetle had stopped moving.

Maybe, she thought, *maybe I should think of this as a survival show.* She'd never actually watched one, but the Dairy Princesses talked about them at rehearsals incessantly. Evidently, people had to eat the oddest things on those shows. And she *was* awfully hungry. Picking up one of the beetles, she popped it into her mouth quickly, before she could think too much about it. But the beetle scrabbled sluggishly on her tongue, which made her gag. She spit it out, scrubbed her hand over her lips, and shuddered violently.

The fox gave a short, sharp laugh, more like a yip. "There are always worms. . . ."

"Starvation is sounding better and better," Moira told him. "Besides, we need to find my friends. I can't believe I slept all night." The light at the cave's entrance was, if anything, brighter. She stood up slowly, being careful not to hit her head.

"There is no rush," the fox said calmly.

"No rush? That monster, that . . ."

"The princesses are to be troll brides, not troll dinner."

"That's a lot of brides," she mused. Then she thought a minute. "I suppose that's . . ." she looked for a word, ". . . preferable to being dinner."

"Very preferable."

Moira wasn't so sure of that. Then she had another

thought. "But the photographer . . . the man. *He* can't be a bride."

The fox looked away and for a long moment said nothing.

Moira squatted down and willed the fox to look back at her. Unbelievably, he did.

"What . . ." she said slowly, spacing out her words for emphasis, as if talking to a slightly stupid child, or a foreigner. ". . . Happened . . . to . . . the . . . man . . . the photographer?"

The fox's black eyes bore into hers. "You do not want to know, human child."

"I do."

"You do not." The fox turned his head away.

Ignoring the fox's warning about being touched, Moira reached out and—as she did with her dog Wolfgang—took his snout in her hand, pulling his head back toward her. "Tell me." No animal, even a talking animal, was going to get the better of her.

He growled and ripped his face away from her grasp. Moira flinched, thinking he would bite her. But he didn't.

"He was eaten," the fox said. Moira paled. "And trolls are notoriously messy eaters."

"Erp," Moira said. Or something like it. A bad taste flooded into her mouth. "I think I'm going to be—"

"Throw up in my cave," the fox said tonelessly, "and I will deliver you to the troll myself."

She gulped back what had already risen into her mouth, and then began to sob.

"Trolls," the fox went on relentlessly, "crave meat. Fresh meat. And human meat most of all. But Aenmarr hasn't had an opportunity to savor any since he made a pact with the humans a long time ago." He bared his teeth. "But you humans broke the pact. Aenmarr must have eaten this meal with gusto."

Sputtering through her tears, Moira cried, "Stop it. I don't want to hear any more."

The fox relented. "I am sorry, child of man. But you did insist on hearing."

"I know. I . . . needed to know." Moira tried to collect her thoughts, but all she could think about was the poor photographer—who she hadn't even known, hadn't even spoken to—stewed or roasted or baked or . . . It was too awful. "I'm a harpist," she managed to say. "Not a hero. And I don't . . . I don't . . . know what . . . I don't know what to do."

The fox smiled and showed too many teeth. "But perhaps," he said, suddenly stretching his head up and licking the tears from her cheeks, an action that was both intimate and frightening, "perhaps I do."

Moira sat down heavily at the fox's feet. "Tell me."

"The first thing you must know," the fox told her, "is that I am a musician, too."

Looking at the creature's paws, she found that hard to believe. They were not built to hold an instrument, much less pluck strings or finger notes.

"Ah, but this is not my true body," the fox said, for he'd read her mind of course. "In that body I look more like a human than an animal, though I am neither. I am a master musician. And I am called Fossegrim."

"Then why be a fox if it is not your true body, Foss?" Moira asked, leaning forward but careful not to touch him again. "It must be hard to play music with . . . with paws."

The fox sighed and gazed wistfully down at his paws, as if recalling a particular lost skill. "Tradition," he answered.

Which, Moira thought, *is no answer at all.* "What do you play?" Really, getting answers out of him was like pulling teeth. She gave a short snort. And he had rather too many teeth.

This time he ignored her thoughts. "I play the fiddle."

Hey-diddle-diddle, the fox and the fiddle. Right! She hated fiddles and country music, that scraping, often off-key sound. Now violins—played with vibrato and passion—that was *real* music. "Where is your . . . fiddle, fox?" She wasn't sure she believed any of this anyway.

"You must open your mind to the world of the impossible," the fox said, "and then it becomes the world of the possible." He shook himself all over. "My fiddle hangs on a wall in Trollholm."

"Okay, Foss," Moira said, a little sharper than she planned. "So you're a master musician who plays a missing fiddle. This will get me to the other girls how?"

"It will get you into Aenmarr's houses. Trolls love music. Well, rather they are transfixed by music. Their taste, however, is execrable and they are never on key."

"Scrabble?"

"Execrable. Bad. Extraordinarily bad."

"Oh." Moira smiled for the first time since arriving at Trollholm. *Execrable* was a good word. It described country music exactly. But as quickly she turned the smile into a frown. "I don't want to get into Aenmarr's house. Not if the troll monster wants me as another of his brides."

The fox sighed in aggravation. "The princesses," he said, speaking slowly in her head as if she—and not he—were the stupid child, "are not to be brides for Aenmarr. He is already married, human child. Do you not know anything? I expect that is why we are in this predicament. The old ones knew about troll brides and sacrifices and . . ."

"Hey!" she interrupted. "You're the one without a fiddle."

He opened his mouth, then snapped it shut again. Taking a deep breath, he said, "The princesses are for his sons."

"He has eleven sons?" That was an awful lot of trolls.

"Oh no, only three."

She thought: *Three I can handle. As long as it's not eleven.*

Foss shook himself all over. "No, child of man, that is three sons too many. One son with each of his wives. Each of whom lives in her own house. Selvi, Trigvi, and Botvi. Aenmarr wants four brides for each son. Troll women only have one child. Not . . ." he said, almost slyly, "like foxes." His eyes suddenly glittered as if he were plotting something.

Moira divided quickly and realized that she was meant to be the fourth bride for one of the troll boys. Had Foss been making more than a simple threat when he said he would deliver her to the troll himself? She let her mind go blank, so as not to broadcast that she guessed this. Foss already knew way too much. Instead, acting innocent, she looked deep into his eyes. "Why me? Why did you save me?"

Foss shifted uneasily on his haunches. "You are a musician. Like calls to like. It is why we can talk, mind to mind.

I cannot speak to the other princesses. They do not have music in their souls. But together you and I will get my fiddle and rescue your friends. And once I have my fiddle . . ." He looked away.

Moira waited to hear the rest. But Foss was suddenly and strangely silent on what would happen after.

· 4 ·

Moira

"Are you ready, human child?" The fox stood.

"Wait," Moira cried, "is it safe?"

Foss stopped, turned his head and said over his shoulder, "Trollholm is never safe. But daylight is less . . . unsafe."

"Oh, great," she said, but he was already gone.

Moira left the cave after him. Outside, red fur gleaming in the sun, he looked like an ordinary fox, certainly quite beautiful, but not magical at all. Glancing past him to a wall of sturdy pines where a path ran between the two tallest trees, Moira whispered, "Maybe . . . maybe we should just go for help. The police. The National Guard. The FBI."

"You cannot leave Trollholm without permission," he told her, the words buzzing inside her head.

"What do you mean, *'permission'*? There's a path." She pointed. "It must lead to somewhere."

"It leads to nowhere, human child. Look more closely. You must open yourself to—"

"To the world of the impossible," she interrupted, but nevertheless she leaned forward and stared at the path and the trees beyond. She saw now what she hadn't noticed before. The path was flat, as if badly drawn, and the trees it ran between were equally flat, unmoving, not fully realized. The whole was like a painting on canvas. *Like the backdrop in a play or an opera.* She'd been in the orchestra for enough stage performances to recognize them. They fooled the eye if the audience gave itself over to the sets. "But how . . . ?" She knew before the fox told her. *Magic.*

Turning, she glared down at him, knowing what to say. "Then give me permission to go."

He laughed that sharp barking laugh again, but this time she heard the pain underneath. "It is not mine to give, child."

Not his to give. That was when she understood. He needed her as much as she needed him. He was a prisoner here, too.

"Then first we get the princesses," she told him. "And then we get the permission."

"No!" He shook his head and his silky red coat trembled with the movement. "First we get the *fiddle.* Once we have that, we can get the princesses, and then . . ."

She didn't believe him. How could she? Balance a fiddle against lives and lives win, every time. Though if it had been a Stradivarius or a Guarneri . . . she knew some violinists who would make the same choice as the fox.

He smiled, showing his teeth. "We have time yet to rescue your friends."

Moira bent over and glared at him, hands on her hips, trying to intimidate him with her size. Alpha female. It worked with her dog. "It may not seem such a big deal to a *fox*," she said, "one who can have lots and lots of *litters*." The way she said *litters* made it sound like garbage on the ground instead of baby foxes. "But human girls are used to dating someone before making up their own minds about the boys, even before they get married. So—"

He cut her short. "Trolls do not date. And they only marry on Frigga's Day," he said. "Today is Woden's Day."

"Who is Frigga and why does she have a day?"

The fox bristled with impatience. "What do they teach human children these days about the gods?" Showing his teeth, he snarled, but the voice in Moira's head was clear. "Have you not heard about the old gods? Frigga was Woden's wife. Woden's Day is what you call Wednesday. Thor's Day, Thursday. Frigga's Day, Friday."

"Oh." Moira nodded slowly. They'd studied that in fifth grade. So, since she'd driven to the bridge after her regular Tuesday rehearsal and had slept overnight in the cave, this would be Wednesday, Woden's Day by Foss' reckoning, which meant they had till Friday. His counting made sense if you believed in talking foxes and trolls. It made sense if you didn't have parents back in Minneapolis and St. Paul calling out the National Guard to look for them.

"We need to go *now*, human child." His words were gentle in her head but she could feel the steel beneath. She recognized it at once, having spent most of her life dealing with musicians, divas, and maestros—all massive egos who always wanted their own way. What was a fox—even a magic fox—compared to them?

She sat down and crossed her legs. "First I need some information."

Foss growled again. "Now."

Moira shook her head. "Before we go anywhere, you need to tell me more about trolls."

"There is nothing more to know. Now move." He began to trot away from her.

She refused to go after him. "All I know," she called out, "is that they have multiple wives and one child each and there's this pact and . . ." She bit her lower lip.

"And they crave fresh meat," he reminded her, his voice in her head cool and commanding.

Fine, she thought and petulantly whistled a middle C—but a full quarter-tone flat. To her trained ear, and, she hoped, to Foss's as well, it sounded horrific. *Chew on that, Master Musician.*

The fox flinched as if struck. Turning his back on her, he spoke abruptly. "Trolls are big, mean, and stupid. More you need not know."

Well, that's something, Moira thought. Then she stood and followed the fox. "At least tell me why it's safer in daylight."

"They sleep," he said.

KEEPING THEIR BACKS TO THE stone cliffs, they walked quickly, quietly. Close up, the stones looked real enough, but from farther away, they too seemed like a flat, painted backdrop. The sky was an impossible blue and the sun a circle of bright orange with rays like a child's drawing.

Moira tried to memorize the direction in which they were going, in case she had to make a swift retreat. No sooner had she thought this, then the sun was hidden behind a thick bank of improbably fluffy gray clouds, so she couldn't tell north from south, east from west. Nor could she figure out what time of day it was. Her watch had stopped, maybe from the fall off the troll's back or maybe watches just didn't work in Trollholm. But since there were no branching paths, she supposed it would be easy enough to find her way back to the safety of the fox's cave. . . .

"My den," he corrected her.

"Get out of my head!"

He shrugged again, the fur rippling down from his shoulders all the way to his tail. Then he trotted ahead about a hundred feet before suddenly stopping at a wide turn in the path.

"There," he said when Moira caught up with him.

Ahead, in an enormous clearing, she saw three similar cottages, each with a high, slanted, thatched roof and gray stone walls. The clearing with the houses seemed as much a stage set as the rest of Trollholm.

"Aenmarr's steading," Foss said. "A house for each wife and son."

"How do you know which is which?" From where they stood, the houses looked alike.

"From the runes on the door, human child. The *great* alphabet," Foss told her. "Each letter a meaning, each meaning full of magic. The human alphabet is a puny thing beside the Futhark Runes." He trotted forward, seemingly unafraid. Crossing the clearing, he went up to the first cottage and stood by the huge wooden door. "Come," he called to her.

Moira was suddenly terrified. "No way. There are trolls here."

"It is daylight. They sleep," he reminded her.

"So you say."

"So I know." He waited by the door, none too patiently, either, cocking his head to one side and tapping his front paw on the ground repeatedly.

You might as well go, she said to herself. *Can't wait here till dark and the trolls wake.* She raced across the clearing toward the cottage on the left, which became more and more real the nearer she got.

When she reached the fox and glanced up at the huge wooden door, she saw that in the middle was a carved letter that looked like a *D,* though what should have been the rounded part was shaped more like a triangle.

"The rune is *Thurisaz,*" Foss said. "It means *giant force of destruction,* the masculine sign. This is Aenmarr's first house where his oldest wife, Selvi, lives." It was the most actual information he'd given her yet.

Selvi's house. With a D for destruction and danger and doom, Moira thought. *I can remember that.*

"We go in," Foss said. "Perhaps my fiddle is here."

"Perhaps?"

"Aenmarr moves the fiddle around, one cottage to another, one wall to another. He seems to think that if the fiddle is where it is happy, it will play for him. He does not understand it takes a musician to make the music."

"Ah." Moira nodded. "Stupid."

"Indeed," Foss said. "Very stupid. Now open the door, human child." He looked at her sideways, his black marble eyes gleaming.

"Just like that?" The door was two stories high and the handle was well above her head. Even if she took a running leap, she wouldn't reach it. There was nothing around to stand on, either, so she glared down at the fox. "Who's being stupid now?"

The fox did not return her stare and Moira wondered if she'd just failed some sort of test.

"Maybe there's an open window," she said. "Or a cat door." Though she'd hate to meet a troll's cat. It would be the size of a tiger.

"Trolls do not like cats," Foss said. He shuddered. Evidently he didn't like them, either.

"I'm checking around back anyway," she told him. "There's no way I can open that door by myself."

"Do what must be done, human child."

Nodding, she left him at the front door. When she rounded the side of the cottage, she saw a window, slightly open from the bottom. It was definitely too high for her to reach, but there was a lovely carved trellis on the side of the house, close by the window. Clearly the troll's wife Selvi had tried her hand at gardening, but all the flowers were dying, with gray, moldy buds hanging like dead men on a gibbet. Stunted brown vines, no more than thin pieces of string, had struggled to get a hold on the lower rungs of the trellis and had never made it. It all looked a bit sketchy, though, and Moira wondered if it would hold her weight. Yet when she got closer, the trellis seemed sturdy enough. Like the rest of Trollholm, it fooled the eye.

Hand and foot, and another handhold. "I'm going up the trellis and in that open window."

"Well, for the gods' sake, be quiet about it," Foss said. "Trolls sleep. But they sleep lightly."

"Now you tell me," she said, already halfway to her goal.

· 5 ·

Moira

Luckily, Moira had no trouble going up. Though coming down carrying a fiddle, might be more of a problem.

"Worry about one thing at a time," urged Foss. But of course he could say that, seeing that he wasn't the one breaking into the troll's house.

About ten handholds up, Moira was finally parallel to the window. From a troll's point of view, it was hardly cracked open at all, just enough to let in some air. But it was open enough for Moira to slip in.

Balancing carefully on the sill, she stared down to a floor that seemed miles below. Luckily there was a heavy red curtain almost entirely obscuring the window. She grabbed hold, as she had the troll's shirt, and hand over hand let herself down.

Slip-slap! Her feet hit the floor and she held her breath, terrified that she'd been heard. Trolls sleep lightly, Foss had said. She had no idea how lightly that meant.

A sudden belch and roar came from a back room. On a table near her a pottery vase filled with dead flowers began to shake. Moira began to shake as well. Another roar rose and fell like an angry wave on a distant shore.

For a moment she was afraid to move, then she broke into silent giggles. The trolls were snoring.

Slowly, she let her breath out and looked around, getting her bearings. The cottage was pretty sparsely furnished, with three chairs, a wooden table, and some hideous skulls of several unidentifiable large animals on the wall, their horns and antlers sticking out in improbable directions. An enormous fireplace with a dark cauldron—big as a hot tub and suspended on an iron arm—took up most of another wall. Along the third wall stood the table with the vase, and next to it a very large wooden box, its top upraised. On the other side of the table was a doorway. The fourth wall had only the window, through which she entered the house, and its dark curtains.

The room smelled like a butcher's shop—musky and meaty. Moira shuddered. She'd been a vegetarian for years. But it wasn't that thick smell that bothered her. It was the fact that there was no fiddle in the room.

Foss, she thought, *what do I do now?*

Unusual for him, he was silent. But she guessed she knew what he'd say: *Check the other rooms.*

Tiptoeing across the floor, she went through a door next to the table. A smaller door on the right led into the larder. A glittering array of knives hung upon the wall, along with some sort of ax and a large fork with three sharp tines.

Shuddering, Moira backed out. She didn't need to see

anything more in that room. Turning, she saw that ahead of her was a larger door, slightly ajar. The belching and snoring had begun again and it hit her like a train coming through a tunnel. Beside the door was a smaller table on which stood a washbasin and a pitcher.

Three beds in graduated sizes stood in the room, and under the covers three snoring trolls. *Papa Bear, Mama Bear, and Baby Bear.* She almost giggled hysterically at the thought.

Get hold of yourself, she warned. The larder and its awful implements were not very far from her mind.

She glanced at the walls of the bedroom. *No fiddle.*

Backing away quickly, she returned to the living room and, as a last thought, checked the large wooden box near the table. In it were four of the Dairy Princesses, lying side by side. Their chests moved steadily up and down and if they weren't dead, they certainly seemed dead asleep.

"Susie . . ." Moira whispered urgently. "Caitlinn . . ."

Nothing.

Moira leaned over and shook Susie's shoulder hard. "Wake up! We have to get out of here."

They slept on.

A loud noise erupted behind her, like footsteps. Her heart hammered in her chest. She looked around wildly for somewhere to hide.

Now heedless of the sound, she ran to the heavy curtains and slipped behind them, her back to the wall. She heard a deep yawn, water trickling into a bowl.

Oh, yuck, she thought, *someone is going to the bathroom.* Only she hadn't seen any bathroom. Just the washbasin. And the pitcher.

Then she heard the footsteps retreating back—she hoped—into the bedroom. Heard a loud yawn. Heard the creak of bedsprings.

She waited a minute, two minutes, five minutes. Then she crept hand over hand up the drapes, which was much harder to do than going down. Reaching the windowsill, she crawled onto it. The air hit her like a fist. She climbed down the trellis, trembling so hard she was afraid she was going to fall.

"Well?" asked Foss. "Any fiddle?"

He's impossible, she thought, not caring that he could hear her.

"No fiddle," she said aloud. "But I saw the girls. Are they . . . are they under some sort of spell?"

He ignored her and trotted away toward the second house. "Fiddle first," he said, which was, as usual, no answer at all.

She had no choice but to follow.

THE SECOND HOUSE HAD A strange looking *P* on the door, the rounded part—like the *D* on the first house—more of a triangle.

"Wunjo," the fox said, gazing up at the rune. "It means *joy* and *comfort* and *pleasure* and *prosperity.* A second wife means a lot to a troll on his own. Aenmarr was very pleased with Trigvi, his next wife, when he made that rune."

Suddenly Moira felt cold. "Are there more male trolls than Aenmarr?"

"Only his sons," Foss said. "Open the door."

This door was as big and as heavy as the other door. Moira ignored Foss and went around the side. Obviously second wife Trigvi was not at all interested in flowers, dead or alive. There was an open window but no trellis.

Moira's heart sank like a boat hitting an iceberg.

"What is an *iceberg*?" asked Foss, trotting behind her.

"Something cold and unmovable," she told him. "Like your heart."

He gave a little yip of a laugh. "Go around the back then."

Around the back was a smaller door with a dung heap by its side. It smelled worse than anything Moira had ever come upon—musky, acrid, foul. She turned and said to Foss, "Roll in that, and we're done."

He drew himself up on his hind legs. "I am not a dog." Then, because the pose was too uncomfortable for long, he dropped down again onto all fours.

Skirting the dump, and refusing to look in it in case she spotted any bones, Moira tried the smaller door. The handle was only slightly above her head. To her relief, she found she could jump up and pull it down. Then by pushing hard against the door with her shoulder, she managed to crack it open a sliver. It was enough, though the door made an awful groan.

Moira stood very still by the open door for a long while, waiting, worrying. She strained to hear, but there was no sound of movement inside. No snores, either.

"Go on . . . go on!" Foss said in her head. "See if the fiddle is here."

To shut him up, she went in.

The door led into the larder, this one more elaborate than the first. Knives hung on the wall, but on an ironwork lattice. An ax lay on the table atop a suspicious dark stain.

As she tiptoed past the table, the door suddenly groaned again and closed with a loud *snick*.

Moira froze, scarcely breathing. From the bedroom, she could now hear light snoring that indicated the trolls—Trigvi and her son—were still sleeping. *But how soundly?*

Going as quickly and quietly as she could, Moira headed into the living room. Another big box sat beside the fireplace. Inside it, Helena and Kimberleigh lay side by side, with Shawneen and Ali next to them, their long princess dresses carefully smoothed down.

"Psssst," Moira tried to wake them, knowing they wouldn't—couldn't—answer. She poked Helena's arm, Kimberleigh's brow. They were as unmoving as the girls in the first box.

Only then did she turn and look at the rest of the room. It was only a little less sparsely furnished than Selvi's house. There was a rag rug on the floor, the colors an unimpressive black and blue. A cloth over the wooden dining table was embroidered with wobbly stitches that looked as if a five-year-old had done it. Where Selvi was a failed gardener, Trigvi seemed to be a wannabe artist.

Above the table, on the wall, was the fiddle. Moira was impressed despite herself. Strange, interlocking patterns were drawn all over the body. Four gleaming strings stretched over the mother-of-pearl inlaid neck, though there were eight tuning pegs. But Moira knew that four more strings ran *under* the neck; she'd seen a fiddle much like this one when she'd played a series of duets two years earlier with Norwegian violinist Arvid Reiersen for a local festival. His instrument had not been quite as beautiful, and boasted a carved head of a maiden as a headstock. Foss', of course, had a fox's head. Its sharp ears pointed toward the fingerboard and black and blue ribbons twined the scroll. The ribbons were so long, they hung down all the way to the floor.

Moira tried to heave the table up against the wall but it wouldn't budge. She stepped back to consider. Even if she managed to get it to move, she'd never be able to climb up onto it. No—the answer was simpler.

She went around the table, grabbed the ribbons, and pulled. It took three tries before the fiddle even began to move on its single nail, and ten more pulls after that before it finally tumbled off. Moira had been terribly afraid she might snap the neck, but clearly it was a magic fiddle and nothing short of a troll's foot on its fingerboard was going to do it any harm. It fell end over end and she caught it in her arms.

Running over to the window, she bound the fiddle to her back using the ribbons, and went hand over hand up the curtains. It was quieter than trying to open the back door again.

Besides, I'm getting good at this, she thought, which surprised her. Gym had never been her best subject.

Foss was waiting below the window as if he had known she would be there.

Of course he knows, she thought. *He's been listening in on my thoughts the whole time.*

She sat on the sill, legs hanging down outside. Carefully,

she unbound the fiddle from her back, and began lowering it to him. When it was halfway down, she noticed something for the first time. Shadows were creeping toward the house from the trees. They looked like cartoon shadows, and moved jerkily.

"Foss," she called softly, "what's happening?"

He stood on his hind legs and grabbed the fiddle with his outstretched paws. Then he placed his mouth around the body of the instrument, as softly as a spaniel picking up a shot bird. Once he held it safely, she dropped the ribbons. The light around him changed, becoming softer, grayer.

His voice came into her head, gentle, sad. "The sun goes down again, human child. Aenmarr wakes to visit his wives." Then he raced away, leaving her alone.

Come back! she cried. *Don't leave me.* She said it only in her head, of course. She didn't dare call out loud. And then she cursed him, with every bad word she knew, which didn't take very long. Only then did she look down at the ground. It was much too far to jump. Especially if Aenmarr was around to hear her.

She looked behind her. Maybe she still had time to get down from the sill, hand over hand, and out the back door.

To her horror, she saw that the back door was now wide open and the troll woman—Trigvi—was bending over, flinging something onto the dung heap. She was huge, but not quite as large as the figure in the water, Aenmarr.

Moira wanted to scream. She wanted to throw up. She wanted to hide her eyes, and weep. But silently she went hand over hand back down the curtain as fast as she could, scrambled over to the box where the other Dairy Princesses lay, climbed in, shoved herself in between Helena and Kimberleigh, and covered herself with their pouffy skirts.

She lay still, trying to slow her frantic breathing. In her mind, she thought she heard a soft barking chuckle. If she were lucky—and her luck had not been very good of late—trolls would be too stupid to count to five.

2 · Brothers Three

∽

Teller, teller, tell me a tale,
Of love and fear and duty,
I want to die in the arms of love,
I want to die for beauty.
For beauty is the only truth,
And death the only lie,
I want to sing a final tale,
And love before I die.

So tell me quick,
If I've been heard,
Else, maim with a phrase,
Kill with a word.

Princess, princess, give me a kiss,
A kiss of love, of pleasure,
I want to lie in the arms of love,
I want to sing of treasure.
For passion is the only truth,
  And death the only lie,

I want to know your lips on mine,
And love before I die.

So tell me quick,
If I've been heard,
Else, maim with a phrase,
Kill with a word.

—Words and music by
Jakob and Erik Griffson
and Moira Darr,
from *Troll Bridge*

Radio WMSP: 10:00 A.M.

"And now, with more on the missing Dairy Princesses, Jim Johnson. Jim?"

"Yes, Katie. More *is not the right word. There's nothing more. And that* is *the story. Despite two days of the biggest manhunt in Minnesota history, with sniffer dogs and everything. . . .*"

"Everything?"

"They've had divers in the river, and that's some cold rushing river, Katie. But police have found no evidence at the site where the twelve Dairy Princesses went missing: the Vanderby Trollholm Bridge."

"What were they doing there, Jim?"

"They were gathered for a photo shoot. They were to stand in the spot where the butter sculptures were normally left."

"Oh, that's right. The heads weren't left there this year were they, Jim?"

"No, Katie, they weren't. The girls' cars have been removed

to the police lab. Aside from those cars, though, there is no evidence whatsoever. No fingerprints, no footprints, no eyewitnesses. Nothing. It's as if the twelve young ladies disappeared off the face of the earth, leaving behind only the butter sculptures of their heads still sitting in the refrigerators at the State Fair."

"Have there been any ransom notes?"

"Nope."

"Phone calls?"

"Nothing that has led anywhere, Katie."

"That's frightening, Jim."

"Very frightening. The police are mystified and there are thirteen desperate families out there just wanting their loved ones home."

"Thirteen, Jim?"

"Don't forget the photographer. Man named Sjogren. He has a wife, stepdaughter, is well liked by his neighbors, a solid citizen. Not even a parking ticket."

"Well, wherever they are, at least the girls will have Sjogren's help."

"His wife says she's sure of that."

"So what's next, Jim?"

"The police say they'll be broadening their search, looking at the boyfriends of the various princesses and any underworld connections."

"And the search at Vanderby, Jim?"

"Groups of concerned citizens have been searching the area from dawn until just before nightfall, Katie, but the police are keeping them well away from the bridge itself. They just don't want the good folk of Vanderby messing up any possible evidence."

"Thanks, Jim—and now here's Bob with sports."

· 6 ·

Jakob

"Dad . . ." Galen Griffson ran his fingers through his hair, something he did only when he was nervous, though the fans all thought it made him look incredibly cool. "Dad . . ."

His father looked up from the pile of papers on his desk and glared at Galen. Jakob could see that glare, could feel it, from the safety of the hallway. As usual, he and Erik were letting Galen do the talking. Front man in their band—and in their lives.

"Dad, we're exhausted. We're going to take a couple of weeks off." Galen's voice had an unfortunate whine in it, Jakob thought. Dad would notice. Would go for his throat.

"Your mother and I are exhausted, too," their father said. "You don't see us taking two weeks off. Where would the band be if we decided to go off on a spree?"

"We're not talking about a spree, Dad."

Uh-oh, bad idea to argue with him, Jakob thought. There was nothing their father liked better than to beat any of them in an argument.

Galen must have realized his mistake and tried a different tack. "Think of the boys," he said. "Think of Erik and Jakob. Especially little Jakob."

Little Jakob is fifteen and a half years old, thank you very much. Jakob glared at his father sitting ramrod straight, the old man's mouth a thin disapproving line. But he realized that Galen was only doing what he always did, putting the blame on younger shoulders when things weren't working out. Because that way Dad would feel sorry for them. Jakob felt like poking Galen in the small of the back with a guitar pick. He could pretty much guess the rest of the sentence, even unspoken. Mom used it all the time and Galen parroted her. *Poor little Jakob with his panic attacks. Poor little Jakob who was in the hospital with pneumonia last year.*

Jakob bit his lip. *Well, rot Galen's hide! Without little Jakob and his little songs, there wouldn't be any Griffson Brothers.* Jakob wasn't really bitter, just realistic. If there was one musician in the family, he was it. The other two just faked it.

He could hear his father shift in his chair. That was a cue for Jakob and Erik to move out of sight, leaving Galen with no backup at all.

"Jakob is fine now," their father was saying. "The wonders of modern medicine. Which leaves you with no excuses, son." The sarcasm was laid on thick. He could maim with a phrase, kill with a word.

For a moment Jakob stopped to consider those lines. *Was there a song to be mined from them?*

Meanwhile, Galen—who hadn't noticed his brothers going AWOL—continued as if they were both there behind him, backing him up. They could hear his voice from down the hall and Jakob realized that Galen had suddenly found real courage. Maybe for the first time.

For a moment Galen continued pleading with their dad. Then suddenly he shifted tactics again. "Whether you like it or not, Dad, we're out of here." His voice was tight, the way it always got at the end of a long set.

Probably, Jakob thought, *Galen's hands are back raking through his hair.* That thick dark fall of hair the girls were all wild about. "Go Gale!" he whispered.

"One week," came their father's voice, full of military authority, as if he were still in the Marines. "You're due in the studio a week from tomorrow. I had to fight for the time as it is. It's then or not for another three months, which we can't afford. You *will* be back then. And return with some new songs. Put your foot down, boy. Make those two come up with something. You're the oldest, the leader. Even if Jakob had to teach you how to play guitar."

Jakob could hear his father's chair scraping on the floor. Having gotten off the killer last line, the interview was clearly over.

Galen escaped out the door without looking back. He walked stiff-shouldered down the hall. When he was far enough from the door, he finally slumped.

Erik got to him first. "My hero!" There was admiration in his voice, along with an echo of their father's sarcasm.

"Let's get out of here. Now!" Galen said. "Before the general changes his mind." Though their father had only been a colonel when he retired, not a general, they all called him that.

"Duffels are packed and in the town car, sir," Jakob told him with a mock salute. "Chocolate, too."

They almost ran out the front door, past the pillars of the fake plantation porch, racing down the five steps as if they'd just robbed the house that their own royalties had bought.

A tune plunged through Jakob's head. Tunes always did that, especially when he was stressed out. He'd been stressed out since he was nine years old and their first record, recorded in their basement on a borrowed ADAT, had been picked up by Virgin Records and gone platinum.

They piled into the car, Jakob in the back with the cooler, Galen in the driver's seat. At nineteen he was the only one of them old enough to drive. Erik would serve as navigator. No roadies, no sound man, no chauffeur. And especially no Mom or Dad. Just the three of them on their own.

How long had it been since that was possible? Jakob couldn't remember. *That's how long.*

"Go! Go! Go!" Erik urged and the motor came alive, purring. Galen swung them around the circular driveway and out along the lake road.

They were free.

THE FIRST FEW MINUTES THEY were all elated, but by the time an hour had passed, elation had given way to a kind of pleasant numbness. They listened to music, mostly Top 40 tunes and spent raucous moments dissing most of it. The shows were interrupted often by odd bulletins about missing Dairy Princesses. Twelve of them, disappeared somewhere north of Duluth. Seemed the girls had gone AWOL two days earlier.

"Maybe we should listen to the news more often," Galen mused.

"Nah . . . too depressing," Erik said, and they both laughed.

Jakob barely paid attention to them. Instead he was staring out the window. As usual, music was running through his head. He tapped on the window in six-eight time, matching the music, and watched the shining expanse of Lake Superior slide past.

Erik noticed the tapping fingers and poked Galen on the shoulder. Then he pointed back at Jakob.

"You got something?" Galen, asked. He looked at Jakob in the rearview mirror.

Jakob nodded at Galen, unruly dark hair with its several cowlicks falling into his eyes as he did. He brushed it away with his left hand. His right kept tapping. He was ambidextrous, a useful trait for a guitar player.

"No words though, right?" Erik asked, a touch malicious, a touch jealous. He never had music come into his head unasked. Even asked, it rarely made an appearance. Just words. Rhymes. Bouncing, bumping, sometimes even inventive. But not music. And all he wanted to do was be able to write tunes that people could sing. He moaned about it all the time.

On the other hand, Jakob reminded himself, *I have music running through my head constantly.* Though, unlike Erik, he could rarely seem to fit words to it. Sometimes a phrase or a line. But only occasionally a whole lyric. Jakob didn't think any of Erik's lyrics were particularly deep, but that didn't stop people from buying their CDs. Enough to go platinum again and again.

And Galen . . .

Well, Jakob thought, *Galen is pretty.* Their mother's high cheekbones, their father's deep dimpled chin, and the only set of teeth in the family that hadn't needed serious remodeling from the orthodontist. Plus the ability to charm audiences single-handedly.

And that, he thought with a wry smile, *is the secret to the Griffson Brothers' success: great music, catchy lyrics, and a real pretty frontman who can kind of, sort of sing and strum the requisite chords.* There were worse boy bands—like all the rest.

He let the new piece of music wash through him. Fingers tapping, he gave himself over to the tune. That's what he did best. And, after all, he didn't need to worry about anything else. Their manager father, their publicist mother, and a whole passel of producers, engineers, sidemen, promoters, sponsors, and roadies took care of the rest, and the music sold in the millions. A teenage boy's dream.

"Dang, I'm tired," Galen said, turning his head a little and smiling that infectious grin.

"*Dang?*" Erik laughed. "We're not being interviewed on TV, Gale. You can actually swear."

Galen grinned some more. "I'm saving it for something big."

"Big as Dad?" Erik teased.

Galen ignored him. "How would you like to drive so I can get some rest, you little pest?"

"Hey, you remember what Dad said, 'Provisional license means *I* set the provisions.'" Erik bellowed the last bit like a drill sergeant. "You know I'm not supposed to drive without him in the car." His hands went up in the air. "But if you're *that* tired." He winked at his big brother.

"We're all tired, Galen," Jakob said. "Just like you told Dad." He knew Galen had only been speaking the truth, the truth the three of them had agreed upon. After all, they'd been touring for eighteen months straight and their father had been getting ready to book them for eighteen more after two months in the studio. Sometimes a dream can become a nightmare. *Well, they now had one week free.* It was more than they'd expected. Their father had never fallen for Galen's charm before.

Galen pulled the car over to the side of the road. "Your turn, kid."

"I'll get my full license in two—" Erik began.

"Two more months and five more days," Jakob broke in. *Two more months and five more days.* Like a lot of musicians, he was mathematically inclined. Erik was nearly seventeen. *Two more months and five more days.* He liked the rhythm of that and a new tune snaked into his head. He liked it even better than the first one.

Meanwhile, Galen got out of the driver's side, Erik out of the passenger's side, and they changed seats.

"Hey, hold on," Jakob called, swinging open his door and jumping out after them. "I've really got something." He ran to the back of the car, then leaned around it and called, "Erik—pop the trunk."

Erik reached down by the driver's seat and pulled up on the little handle. Once the lock clicked, Jakob lifted the trunk door, then dug around, tossing duffels and sleeping bags aside until he found his guitar. Only the one instrument. His brothers had left theirs at home. "This is a vacation," Erik had said. "Why would I want to bring my work tools along?"

But Jakob was never without his guitar any more than he could be without one of his limbs. Pulling the Taylor from its case, he sat on the back bumper, strumming chords, searching for the right key.

Erik got out again and strolled around the car. "All right," he said. "Let's hear it."

Jakob didn't respond. He had found the key, and was playing what was in his head. Six-eight and major, the melody danced on the high strings while he plucked a walking baseline on the low E with his thumb.

"That's really good," commented Galen. Jakob hadn't even noticed him come up. "Sounds kind of old timey."

"Yeah." Erik cocked his head to one side, thinking. "Needs some contemporary lyrics to set that off. Something out of the news." He listened for a minute more.

Jakob changed keys for a bridge, then drifted back into the main theme.

"I've got it!" Erik said. "That news story we just heard on the radio." He began to sing to Jakob's tune.

Twelve dairy princesses, where did they go?
Twelve dairy princesses, I'd really like to know.

The Devil snatched them from thin air
So they couldn't make it to the fair
And now's he's gone and taken them below.

Erik's voice had just finished its change, and it sounded pretty rough. But Jakob knew Galen would probably be the one to sing this song, anyway. The lighter, funnier songs were his. He couldn't carry a really beautiful ballad but was perfect with the humorous tunes. Jakob honestly liked the words so far. They were topical—but had imagery, too.

And he was singing:
What's better than a butter girl?
Badder than my better girl.
Best when I'm not buttered up as well.
What's better than a butter girl?
Badder than my better girl.
Best that I just take them all to Hell.

Jakob sighed. *So much for liking the lyrics,* he thought. *But that's probably the part of the song everyone will sing along to. It'll be our next big hit: "The Badder Better Butter Girl."* Especially if the girls are found. His dad would probably do a deal with the Dairy Princesses and get them to dance on the video in their tiaras and long dresses and . . .

Galen had caught the melody now and was roaring out the butter girl chorus with Erik who had shifted to harmony, which, even with his rough voice, sounded pretty good.

And then, Jakob thought, *I'll hate it. Hate it like all the others.*

He played the song twice through, knowing that the tune, at least, wouldn't change at all now that he had it firmly in his hand. He'd never forget it.

Head and hand. That's how his music was stored. His mother hired transcribers to write it down for them. Write the music down and package it into thin books that sold to teenage boys just starting to strum. But that was just another piece of the Griffson moneymaking machine.

Jakob certainly never looked at the books. He had no need to. And Galen couldn't read music well enough to use them. Erik, either. And they wouldn't write this one down for a while yet. There was sure to be another verse or two, whatever happened to those poor missing girls, gone to Hell—or wherever.

· 7 ·

Jakob

Back in the car, Jakob stared out the window, idly strumming his guitar and singing the butter girl song softly. His voice occasionally broke, which still embarrassed him. He'd had a gorgeous falsetto until last year.

"Where are we going?" He didn't recognize the landscape. But then he never noticed such things. Life on the road was like that. Travel dulled all his senses, especially his sense of direction.

Now in the front passenger seat, Galen turned around. "Why, we'll do what Mom and Dad used to do when we were younger. We'll go without a plan. You've probably just forgotten."

Jakob tried to remember a time when they hadn't been traveling for a purpose. Get to a gig, a talk show, a press conference.

Banging a hand on the steering wheel, Eric added, "We just figure it out as we go along, little brother."

"That's right!" Galen crowed. He ran a hand through his hair. "We're leaving Duluth now. Heading up the North Shore." He paused. "Looking for oddballs and oddities."

Not one to miss an opportunity at alliteration and word-play, Erik said, "Chaos and carnivals!"

Galen looked over his shoulder expectantly, and Jakob suddenly remembered the word their parents had always given to describe their early journeys, all five of them and their gear stuffed into an old station wagon, going where a sunset or a river or an odd old barn led them. A word they'd used before fame and fortune overtook them.

"Serendipity," he said. "Surprise and serendipity." As he said it, a new song burst into his fingers, and he gave himself over to it. Galen glanced back at him and then exchanged knowing smiles with Erik, but Jakob didn't notice. He was caught by the muse and played frenetically for nearly an hour before placing his guitar gently on the seat next to him, and dropping into an exhausted slumber.

JAKOB WOKE WITH A FUNNY snort. The sun was sinking behind the trees, and the sky shone with a red-orange glow. The car was inching along. "What's going on?"

He released his seat belt and leaned forward, peering out the windshield. They were no longer on a major road, in fact they were hardly on a road at all, only a dirt drive with barely enough room for two cars to pass. Pine trees crowded the roadside, leaning over as if trying to peek into the car.

Erik spun the wheel sharply and the car turned left onto an even smaller path.

"Wow!" Galen exclaimed.

A short distance ahead was a clearing with yellow police ribbons, like tattered banners, all around, but no policemen in sight.

"That's bizarre," Erik said.

At one end of the clearing lay a small stone bridge arching over a river. The bridge appeared old enough to have been built by the first Norwegians to enter Minnesota. Pocked and lichen-covered, the bridge was lined with low stone walls. At either end stood stone gargoyle sentries, slope-shouldered, gape-mouthed, and hideous.

"Look!" Jakob said, pointing. Directly in the middle of the bridge sat the largest fox he'd ever seen. Bright cinnamon and bushy-tailed, it was in profile to the car. Slowly it turned its head to stare at them. The fox's eyes were jet black, but Jakob was sure it was looking right at him. It had to do with the way its head cocked to one side, then slowly straightened, its eyes never leaving his. Then, giving its head one dip, the fox leapt to its feet and dashed toward the far side of the bridge.

Follow. The word popped into Jakob's head unbidden. As if in a trance, Jakob said aloud: "Follow!"

"The fox?" Galen asked.

Jakob nodded.

The fox stopped abruptly and looked back at the car.

Follow, came the thought again, and again Jakob said "Follow."

"Why?" Galen asked.

Jakob shook himself. "Follow it! Just follow the stupid fox, okay?"

Galen glanced at the setting sun. "Cool it, little brother. It's getting dark. We should go back to the main road and find somewhere to stay for the night. Besides, look at those yellow ribbons. Something bad's happened here."

Erik laughed. "The Dairy Princesses happened here. That's *my* serendipity!"

"Or un-happened here," Galen added. He laughed, shivered, laughed again.

"So where are the cops?" Erik asked.

"It's almost night. They have to sleep sometime," Galen said.

"Erik," Jakob said. "Follow the fox."

"Why?"

"Because . . . because that's why we're on this trip, right? He's *my* serendipity!" He poked Erik in the shoulder. "Follow!"

All of a sudden, Galen looked stern. Lines formed on his forehead. "Erik. No."

"Aw, Galen," Erik said. "You sound just like Dad." Then, grinning from ear to ear, he dropped the car into drive. "All right, little brother. Let's go." He stomped on the gas and the car surged forward toward the bridge.

The fox saw them coming and raced away, its tongue lolling out of its mouth.

The bridge's bottom surface was not macadam but cobblestones, and the town car's wheels rattled alarmingly as they rolled onto it.

Sitting back, Jakob clicked his seat belt back into place. He placed a hand protectively on his guitar.

"Hey!" Galen yelped. "Slow down, idiot!"

Erik just grinned. "Why should I?"

Galen punched him in the shoulder. "Because you'll hit the fox, dummy."

Jakob stared ahead. They were at the middle of the bridge, and there below them, at the bridge end, sat the fox idly licking its forepaw.

"It'll move," Erik said.

It didn't have to. A sudden surge of dark water as high as a two-story house washed over the car.

"What the . . ." exclaimed Galen.

Jakob screamed in terror, and Erik grabbed tight to the wheel, trying to keep the car under control.

Then the car was inexplicably in midair.

Jakob shut his eyes tight, whispered a quick prayer, and braced himself for impact. None came.

After a moment, he opened his eyes again. The windows were water-blurred, but he swore he could see a giant greenish hand holding the car by the roof. Jakob blinked, willing the nightmare away. Attached to the giant hand was a giant hairy greenish arm. He blinked again. At the end of that, a naked hairy, slope-shouldered torso, on top of which stood a thick neck. A giant head balanced there, large as a VW bug. It was warty and swamp green, two yellowing teeth poking out of a malicious grin. Jakob blinked a third time, figured he was hallucinating. Or dead.

"Hello, my pretty young princes," the creature said in a deep rumble that echoed inside the car. Then it heaved back its arm and dashed the car against the rocks by the riverside. Airbags inflated, and the windshield exploded into a massive spiderweb. Hard kernels of glass showered over Jakob. He tried to shout, tried to scream again, but he couldn't seem to catch his breath.

"Jakob?" Galen called in a panic.

Jakob couldn't answer. His throat simply wouldn't make a sound.

"Erik?" Galen cried.

But Erik was gone. He hadn't been wearing his seat belt and had been thrown clear. That much Jakob could see. He worked frantically at his own buckle. *Have to get out. Have to get out.* The words kept repeating in his mind. He finally popped the latch and fell painfully onto his neck and shoulders. The car was upside down.

Somehow finding his voice again, Jakob screamed. But there was no one left to respond. The front seat was now empty.

"Galen?" Jakob called in a panic. No answer. Rolling over, he tried to open the back door. It was stuck. He put his shoulder to it, a weak effort, but surprisingly the door flew open. Flew off in fact. And there was the giant green creature, holding the door in one massive hand, and an unconscious Erik and a squirming Galen in the other.

"There you be, young prince." He snorted and his fetid breath filled the car with the smell of rotting meat.

And butter, Jakob thought, scuttling backward, but too late.

The creature dropped the door with a clang, and reached into the car to wrap his hairy fingers around Jakob's waist. Jakob scratched and clawed at the hand, but he didn't even break the surface of the rough green skin.

Even in his panic, Jakob thought: *My guitar!* He reached out to snag the instrument by the neck and managed a small sigh of relief that it appeared undamaged. But his relief was short-lived as he was suddenly dragged from the upside-down car, his back catching painfully on the ceiling light.

When Jakob was entirely out, the creature lifted his hands in front of his face and eyed the three boys, nodding with satisfaction.

Jakob twisted around and glared down at the fox who was still sitting at the end of the bridge, staring up at him with sad dark eyes and, inexplicably, nodding.

You . . . you set us up! Jakob thought at the fox. *Why?*

Before the fox could answer, the giant creature laughed aloud, a sound so human that it was startling. Then, with the boys clutched in his enormous hand, he dove straight into the river. Jakob felt the black waters engulf him, and he fainted dead away.

· 8 ·

Jakob

Jakob awoke with a splitting headache. He tried to figure out where he was, but his head was spinning too badly for him to make any sense of what he saw. It took him a moment before he realized what was wrong.

I'm upside down! And it wasn't his head that was spinning. It was his whole body.

His feet had been tied together with thick rope, and the knot thrown over a large hook, so that he hung from the ceiling by his bound feet, rotating slowly. His hands were shackled behind him. As he spun, he caught isolated details of the room he was in: a stained wooden table, a poorly constructed chair, some haunches of meat hanging next to him. He groaned. For a moment it was all he could manage.

Finally he took a deep breath. "Where am I?" *That came out in such a weak, puling way,* he thought stupidly, *my singing teacher would hate it.*

"Trollholm!" came the immediate answer. "You be in Trollholm." That voice was deep and gruff, but somehow still childlike.

Mercifully, Jakob's spinning stopped as someone grabbed his shoulder. He looked into the upside-down face of another green-skinned creature, like the one from the bridge, but much smaller, barely twice Jakob's size.

"Who . . . what . . . are you?" Somehow he was afraid he might know. But if he was right, than he had to be dreaming. Asleep in the car and dreaming. Or dead. Because what he was thinking didn't happen in the real world. Not the world of cars and planes and rock-and-roll.

"Me? Me? Why, I be a troll, of course!" the creature said.

"Of course," Jakob said. "Fol-de-rol." It was a song from his childhood. And this was a nightmare out of that same childhood.

"And what be you?" the troll asked.

Jakob thought for a minute, or as long as his aching head allowed. The troll didn't seem very bright. "*Not* a troll?" It was pretty weak for an answer.

But the troll seemed to find it hilarious, and with a yellow, gap-toothed grin, gave Jakob a swat so hard he knew it was no dream. The swat sent him spinning again.

"Oddi!" someone called from the next room. "Stop playing with your food!"

The troll sighed. "Yes, Mother." Then he skipped out of the room through an oval door, leaving Jakob dizzy and alone.

Alone! Jakob gulped. If he were alone, where were his brothers. Escaped? Drowned?

Or already eaten.

He took a deep breath. Trolls, it seemed, had very big and yellow teeth. And probably very big appetites. Even—*it appeared*—the little ones. That was all he knew so far.

And then he realized he knew something more. Trolls—at least little ones—weren't very bright. Maybe even . . . stupid. *Stupid.* He could do something with stupid. If he could only get his hands free. And his feet. And stop the rope from spinning.

Jakob wriggled his hands behind him. They were firmly fastened at the wrists. By gritting his teeth and working hard, he managed to squeeze himself up into a sitting position, something an Olympic gymnast might have admired, his face right next to the ropes binding his feet. His stomach muscles burned with the effort.

What now, though? he thought. He had to hurry before the troll kid came back. Had to get free. But his hands were still bound, and the ropes at his feet were too thick to chew through. Jakob tried anyway. The rope tasted like a burlap sack, and he didn't make any headway at all before his strained stomach muscles gave up and he collapsed upside down once again. Blood rushed back into his head, and it started throbbing anew.

"Owwwww!"

Jakob tried to ignore the pain in his head, the burning in his stomach, and when the muscles finally relaxed a bit, he forced himself to sit up again. This time, he grabbed a piece of the knot in his teeth, and tried to work it loose. The knot didn't budge, and Jakob collapsed once more, panting heavily now.

Voices filtered in from the next room.

"I be going to gather vegetables, Oddi," the mother troll roared in a voice like a freight train. It was super loud as if she had only one tone. "When your father be returning, it be into the stew pot with yonder prince."

Jakob didn't like the sound of that at all. Redoubling his efforts to undo the knot, he nearly took his front teeth out. But the knot remained stubbornly whole.

"And Oddi," the mother troll continued in her unrelenting voice, "don't be going into the larder again!"

"Yes, Mother," Oddi replied, but there was mischief in his answer. As soon as the door slammed behind her, he skipped back into the room where Jakob was hanging.

"Mothers!" the troll said and giggled. Then he noticed Jakob spitting out rope fiber in disgust.

Oddi looked at him, eyes wide. "What be you doing?"

Jakob thought furiously, but only managed to come up with the plainest of truths "Eating rope," he said.

"Why? Does it taste good? Should I be trying?"

Very stupid, Jakob thought, thankfully. He spit out the last bits. "Why," he said as calmly as he could, "I'm trying to fatten myself up. I'm hardly a meal for three trolls at this size, am I?" He hoped the answer was no.

Oddi looked him up and down hungrily. Then he reached out and pinched Jakob's arm. Jakob bit his lip to keep from crying out. The pinch felt as if it went right to the bone.

"I suppose not," Oddi said slowly. But he didn't sound convinced.

"Well, didn't your father bring two others like me in? Only bigger?"

Oddi nodded enthusiastically. "Oh, yes. My father said he be out of practice hunting, what with the Compact and all. But I think he be doing fine, don't you?"

Jakob didn't understand what the troll was talking about, but he figured it was better to be agreeable, so he nodded back just as enthusiastically. "Absolutely." Then, because it made his head hurt worse than ever, he stopped nodding. Trying to sound nonchalant, he added, "What happened to the other two?"

"Two?"

"Two princes," Jakob said. It was like making conversation with a bowl of Jell-O. Green, stinky, dangerous Jell-O.

"Oh, them." Oddi frowned. Of course, from Jakob's angle, it looked like a smile. And not a pleasant smile at that. "They be taken to father's older two wives."

He sounds a little jealous, Jakob thought. "Do the other wives have children?"

Oddi nodded, his frown deepening. "Two boys. One each. Older than me."

If he weren't green already, Jakob thought, *I believe he'd be turning that color, now.* "So, your half brothers get the big tasty morsels, while you're stuck with scrawny little me?"

"Yes!" Oddi grunted. A hippo grunt, not a pig grunt. "It be not fair." He stomped a big green foot and gave Jakob a petulant swat that sent him spinning again.

Jakob's head was pounding insanely. He fought hard not to pass out and instead said calmly as he spun, "I . . . know . . . how . . . you . . . feel . . . I . . . have . . . two . . . older . . . brothers . . . too." And strangely, he did understand

Oddi. Sometimes, it was tough being the youngest. Watching your older siblings getting bigger and better stuff than you; watching them doing things you weren't allowed to yet.

Oddi eyed him suspiciously. His big green lower lip trembled. Then he grabbed Jakob's head in one of his big hands, stopping him spinning and almost snapping his neck.

"Maybe I can help you," Jakob said with an effort.

Oddi pulled Jakob forward until they were nearly nose to nose. "How?" he asked.

Almost overwhelmed by the stinking breath, Jakob forced himself to stare unblinking into the troll's big green eyes. *Yeah,* he thought. *How indeed?*

Apparently, Jakob was silent for too long, because Oddi pulled a hand back to swat him again.

"Wait! We can . . . um . . . ." Jakob thought hard. "We can trade places."

Oddi stopped with his hand in the air, a hand that was filthy, dirt-encrusted. He stuck the finger into one giant nostril as if that helped him think. "Trade places?" he said at last.

"Yes. I can trade places with one of the bigger princes." Jakob tried to smile reassuringly. It turned out to be hard to smile upside down. "Who would know but you and me?"

"Hmmmm," Oddi hummed, pulling the finger out again, "That might be working."

Jakob told himself. *Don't sound too eager.* Then he smiled in what he hoped was a friendly manner. "You'll have to get me down first."

Oddi nodded happily. Grabbing Jakob by the shoulders, he heaved upward till Jakob's feet were free of the hook.

Then he tossed him over his shoulder like a sack of potatoes and made for the door.

"Wait!" Jakob cried, desperation overcoming caution. "Won't your mother be angry if she comes back and finds you gone?"

Oddi thought a moment. "I . . . I suppose she be very angry. We be having to hurry."

"You'll never make it back in time."

Oddi sniffed despondently. "What can we be doing?" He set Jakob on the floor.

We? Good, we're a team now. Jakob made his voice calm, authoritative, adult. He looked up at the troll. "Untie me," he said, "and I'll run to your father's other house, and trade places, sending my bigger brother back here."

Oddi looked doubtful, his big eyes scrunching up into half-moons, his finger once again in his nostril.

Jakob said gently, "Remember—you'll be getting the big meal, and your half brother only a snack. I know the prince I'll trade with. His name is Erik." Jakob dropped his voice to a conspiratorial whisper. "And he's *fat*!"

A spot of drool formed at the corner of Oddi's mouth and tendrilled grotesquely to the floor. "Fat," he breathed.

Oddi quickly untied Jakob's hands and Jakob slipped his feet free of the rope then rubbed them briskly to try to get some feeling back.

"Wait a minute! Wait a minute!" Oddi cried. "I just be thinking of something."

Jakob broke into a sweat. He looked around for a weapon. Although there were plenty—enormous knives, cleavers, axes hanging from pegs on the larder wall—he doubted he could heft a one. But that didn't matter anyway because he didn't get a chance to move a single step toward any of them before Oddi grabbed his shoulders in a crushing grip.

"My mother be just as angry to find *you* gone," Oddi said. "Maybe even more so."

Jakob was speechless. The little troll was stupid, but not—it turned out—quite stupid enough. *So close to freedom,* Jakob thought, *and still so far.*

Jakob clenched his puny fists and prepared to do battle. But instead of retying Jakob's feet and hands, the troll said, "I be knowing what to do." He had a strange look on his face, somewhere between a grin and a dropped jaw. Then he stepped back, and with a wave of his warty hand, disappeared.

In his place, stood . . . Jakob.

Jakob looked at his mirror image, mouth agape. "But . . . but . . ." He couldn't figure out what had just happened.

"Hurry," Oddi said in Jakob's voice. "Be tying me. Before mother be back." He chortled. "Oh, this be great fun!"

Some fun, Jakob thought, *especially if it leads to the stew pot.* But he was careful not to say that aloud. Instead, he shook himself from his trance, and grabbed the ropes. Looped a piece around his—*er . . . Oddi's*—feet and tied a fat knot. Then he tied the troll's hands, examining the left hand carefully. *No guitar-playing calluses on his fingertips. Not as exact a copy as it first appears.*

"All right, prince, now be hanging me from the hook!"

Jakob considered just running, what with the troll tied up and all. But he didn't know if Oddi could change back again. Maybe he needed to wave his arms around, and maybe he didn't. So Jakob figured the longer Oddi held his enchantment, the more time Jakob had to escape and save his brothers. So, wrapping his arms around the disguised troll, he gave a giant heave.

Oddi didn't budge.

Jakob tried again. It was like trying to lift a truck. The troll might look like Jakob, sound like Jakob, even (thank God) *smell* like Jakob. But . . .

"You must weigh a thousand pounds."

"It be called a *seeming,*" the troll said, as if that explained everything.

And maybe it does, Jakob thought. The troll only seemed to be Jakob, but wasn't. He wondered if he should just try running.

"Oh," Oddi said. "Be standing back, prince. I be having another idea."

Jakob stepped away and watched in astonishment as the troll crouched low, then launched himself upward in a perfect backflip. At the apex of the leap, Oddi hooked his feet over the ring, and hung upside down, swaying back forth. He winked at Jakob.

Jakob was too astonished to wink back.

"My parents be returning soon. I be hungering for this fat companion of yours." His upside-down grin was like a gargantuan frown. "Run, little prince, run!"

"You know," Jakob said, "I'm not really a prince . . ."

"Of course you be a prince," Oddi said. "Only princes be trying to rescue princesses." Then he grinned and said again, "So run, little prince."

Jakob finally ran, making for the oval door. But he stopped before opening it, turned around. "Which way do I go?" he asked.

"You go . . ." Oddi began, but then he stopped and cocked one ear forward. "Uh-oh."

That's when Jakob heard a deep, grumbling jet plane kind of voice from the other side of the door.

"Family! It be I, Aenmarr, come to eat my first meal of the evening."

Jakob

Jakob jumped away from the door, in a full panic now. *What to do? What to do?* There were no other exits to the room and the only place to hide was under the rough wooden table. He glanced around frantically for one second more, then scuttled underneath, crouching in the shadow of one of the back legs, and praying it would conceal him.

"Wife? Son? Where be you?"

"Ooh, Father be home," Jakob heard himself say. No, it was Oddi speaking from overhead but in Jakob's voice now. "I think we be in trouble."

I'm not in any more trouble than when I was before, tied and hanging upside down. Jakob grabbed his knees to stop his shaking as he listened to the thumping footsteps approaching. Then the door swung open and two gigantic bare green feet stomped into the room. The toenails were long and yellow and caked with dirt. They looked more like claws.

"Hmm," the father troll rumbled. "Aenmarr be home but all alone. Botvi must be taking Oddi with her to gather vegetables." Jakob heard a metallic scrape as Aenmarr pulled a tool off the wall. "I be starting the preparations without them."

There was a sudden *whoosh* and a *thwock*. Then a thud sounded behind Jakob and he turned to see his own head lying on the floor, staring at him with lifeless eyes. Bile rose in Jakob's throat.

Puke and you die, he told himself, knowing that the noise of it would make Aenmarr look under the table. He swallowed hard.

There was another thud above him, as something heavy hit the table. Then there came a disconcerting assortment of chopping, slicing, snapping, grinding, squishing, squelching, and other revolting sounds.

Jakob bit his lip and covered his mouth with his hand, trying with all his might to keep his food in his stomach where it belonged.

That could be me, he reminded himself. *It still might be. Me—or my brothers.* He kept quiet as Aenmarr continued his gruesome work. *I have to save them,* he thought fiercely. But as the minutes stretched on and his mind created visions to match the sounds above him, he realized something. *Whatever happens, I can't cause the death of anyone else.*

Apparently finished, Aenmarr gave a loud cry of, "To the pot!" and stomped out of the room.

A door squeaked open. "Husband, I be home. Be you seeing Oddi?"

"I be seeing only the prince in the larder. He be in the pot stewing." Aenmarr chuckled, a noise like a lion snorting. "We be going to the dining room to have ourselves a feast."

NOT AN HOUR LATER, KNEELING by the big oval door, Jakob listened to the sounds of Aenmarr and Botvi eating their son for dinner.

"By the rotting bones of Thor," Aenmarr's voice was a deep, contented rumble, "this be the best stew I be eating in centuries."

Jakob heard a slurp.

"I believe you be right, husband," Botvi replied. "But where be our son, Oddi, to enjoy this meal with us?"

"I be not knowing this. But I be having the hide off of him if he be not here by daybreak." Aenmarr gave a roaring chuckle. "Or if he be stupid enough to stay out in the sun, I be putting him in the garden for the birds to perch on!"

"Aenmarr! Do not jest. I be worrying about him."

"I be finding him, Botvi. But only when dinner be done." A great belch shook the door. "When *all* my dinners be done."

"Bah!" Jakob heard the scrape of a chair being pushed back. "All you do be eat, husband. I be finding Oddi myself. *Before* sunrise."

There were footsteps and the sound of a door creaking open, then slamming. Aenmarr grunted. "All you be doing is complaining, wife. I be going to Trigvi's next. Perhaps she be more even-tempered." Jakob heard Aenmarr's chair sliding back. "*Huldres* when you woo them, and hags once you marry." His voice was growing softer as he moved away, like thunder from far off. "As sure as the sun turns you to stone."

Jakob heard the sound of the door creaking open again, but no slam. Then silence.

Collapsing against the larder door, Jakob breathed a deep sigh. *Safe. For now.* His underarms were slick with sweat, the same way he sweated when a gig went bad. The walls of the troll's house seemed to be pressing in on him. It was a panic attack. He could taste the fear in his mouth, that awful iron taste.

Oh God, no, he thought, trying to force himself to breathe slowly. Not now. He had to move. He had to think about his brothers. He had to breathe. Aenmarr was surely on his way to this Trigvi's to eat one of them.

Forcing himself to his feet, Jakob yanked on the big oval door. It was heavy as a tombstone, but creaked open. He peeked in. The room was unadorned. There was only a single long rough-carved wooden table with three large stoneware bowls on it, only one still containing any stew. Three high-backed wooden chairs sat around the table. A fire crackled in a fireplace that was as big as the ruined town car. And high up on the far wall, suspended by two wooden pegs tucked under its headstock, was Jakob's guitar.

He rushed over to get it down, but it was hanging too high up to reach. So he tried to haul one of the huge chairs against the wall.

It's like trying to move a piano!

For a moment he stared critically at his guitar, as if blaming it for hanging up so high. Then he sighed. *Probably couldn't reach it even if I managed to get the chair over there, anyway.*

As he passed the huge fireplace, he noted the bathtub-sized cauldron suspended over the flames by a long iron bar. Vile smelling liquid popped and bubbled over the sides. Jakob thought of Oddi and gagged.

No sicking up, he warned himself. He wondered if any of his childhood heroes—King Arthur, Spider-Man, Stevie Ray Vaughn—had ever felt this way. His mouth twisted wryly. None of them had ever encountered a troll.

He found another door, a huge thing two stories high that wasn't shut completely, and listened a minute, afraid he might hear the trolls returning. When he heard nothing, he pushed the door open another crack—which was a feat in itself as it was like moving a truck—and found himself outside.

It was night. Pitch black.

They can't see me. I can't see them. Good news, he thought, *and bad.*

The heavy door creaked closed after him. He wondered if Oddi's mother, Botvi, was still out looking for him. And he wondered how good troll ears really were. He was afraid he'd find out all too soon.

"Oddi?" he heard Botvi calling out in her freight train voice. "Be that you?"

Yep, Jakob thought, *I've found out way too soon.* He scrambled away from the door, panicked and blind in the pitch dark.

"Where you be running to, my son?" Botvi said, closer now. "Hold still, you be looking so strange."

Oh no! he thought. *Of course trolls can see in the dark. It's sunlight they can't stand.* Reaching out his hand, he trailed it along the rough stone of the house until he reached the corner and the wall dropped away. Then he darted around the side of the house and—he hoped—out of sight. Charging off into the darkness, he ran as fast as he could. Maybe his eyes were adjusting to the dark, because after a bit he began to distinguish actual shapes against the general flat, depthless black. He tripped over the first—a humped-up tree root.

"Oooof!" he grunted. He hauled himself to his feet and stumbled on, aware that if he weren't more careful, he'd be . . . troll dessert.

Suddenly a shadow loomed in front of him and his feet tangled in it. He reached out to stop himself from falling again, only to discover the thing was furry, some sort of animal. Flinging himself to one side, he tumbled to the ground.

"Oddi? I be growing angry." Botvi had turned the corner of the house, too, and Jakob could hear her footsteps coming nearer. "Be stopping your foolery this instant."

Jakob started to scramble to his feet, but froze when he heard a low growl right in front of him. He squinted into the dark. A set of bright white, almost phosphorescent, fangs gleamed inches from his face.

"Um," he gulped. "Nice doggy?" he pleaded in a whisper while pushing himself backward on his belly. *Toward the troll!* Reconsidering quickly, he kicked forward, only to be brought up short by another growl. And the teeth.

Isn't this a pretty pickle, he thought, then in a hysterical afterthought he wondered if trolls ate pickles with their meals.

But the teeth disappeared. Or rather the creature that owned the teeth closed its mouth. Shook its dog-sized head. *Dog?* he thought before noticing it had a longer, pointier nose than a dog. And as he stared at it, the animal very clearly shook its head at him.

It's a fox, he thought. Then, *No, it's the fox. The one from the bridge. The one that got us into this mess to begin with!* At that, his hysteria rose again, like a vampire from a coffin, because he just remembered that *mess* was a soldier's word for *dinner.*

The fox bared its teeth again, but for some reason, Jakob was sure that this time it was more of a grin than a threat. Then with a short bark, the fox dashed past him.

Sic 'er! Jakob thought as the fox headed toward Botvi.

"Bah!" she cried almost immediately, throwing something in his direction. "Away with you, ill-omened creature. I be thinking you be Oddi."

The fox ran off yipping, and Jakob stayed frozen on his belly, praying the he was somehow hidden from sight. Evidently Botvi was only as smart as a troll, and she turned and walked back the way she'd come, her bass drum footsteps quickly fading. "I be wasting my time chasing after foxes," he heard her say, "when my dear son be lost."

Jakob suddenly thought about his own mother and what she'd say when the smashed car was found. *If* it was found. *Nothing,* he reminded himself, *can be counted on if there are trolls in the world.* He would have cried—for his own mother, for his father, for his brothers . . . but he didn't have time. He only allowed himself a deep sigh of relief and a whisper. "Thanks, fox." He heard an answering yip.

"Now," he said under his breath, "how do I find my brothers?"

· 10 ·

Jakob

Jakob took a chance and stood up. He could see nothing. The dark in this place was deeper than anything he'd ever experienced. No moon or stars overhead, which was odd, as the sky seemed cloudless.

He turned around slowly.

No light shining through troll house windows or open doors.

Nothing. Nothing but the deep dark and . . . He banged the flat of his hand dramatically against his forehead. *Of course!*

"No light through windows," he whispered to himself, "because if they forget to close the shutters and morning comes, the sunlight could accidentally turn them to stone." But that realization got him nowhere fast. And fast was what was needed if his brothers were to be rescued. Aenmarr could now be at his second wife's house, in the larder, taking Erik or Galen off the hook and using one of the big knives to—

He felt a heavy stone in his chest.

Stop it! he scolded himself, *or you'll bring on a real panic attack, a can't-move-blinding-throw-up-no-breath attack.* He forced himself to breathe slowly until he was calm again. *You aren't a troll, and you have a brain.* He just had to use it.

Turning in a slow circle once more, staring into the blackness, he thought: *What good is a brain, if you've nothing to feed it with?*

He almost shouted out, "I can't see anything!" but caught himself before making any noise. He certainly didn't want Botvi to hear him and come back.

That's it! Jakob thought. *Hearing.* He closed his eyes—not that he could see anything anyway—and shut out everything so he could concentrate on sound alone, letting his ears do their work. After all, he could tune a guitar to open C without an electric tuner. He could guide multitudes of backup singers through three- and four-part harmonies. He could hear missed notes in string sections that even the top producers in L.A. didn't notice. *Listen!* he told himself. *What do you hear?*

He stood motionless.

There's the buzzing of insects. The sigh of the wind. And rushing water? Yes, rushing water, but a long way away.

Cocking his head to one side, he tried to listen harder. His brothers' lives depended on it. And, like eyes adjusted to the dark, after a few moments it was if Jakob's ears adjusted to the silence. He heard not just the pick-buzz of insects, but the dozens of different songs and calls they made. The wind didn't just sigh, it thrummed and whistled and whirred, rustling through the leaves of nearby trees and the thatch of the roof.

There! A barely audible sound, off to his right, that wasn't insects or wind or water. A metallic swish, not natural. But something he'd heard before. Jakob opened his eyes and began moving even as he tried to place the sound. For some reason, it made him think of Thanksgiving.

Thanksgiving, he thought. *Why Thanksgiving?*

Jakob suddenly pictured his father in the kitchen, a turkey set out on a carving platter next to him. In his hands, a big knife and a metal stick for . . .

For sharpening the knife!

Hands held out in front of him, Jakob burst into a sprint despite the darkness. He knew what that sound meant. It was doom. Aenmarr the Troll was in the larder of his second wife's house and he was sharpening his knives.

"Oh God, oh God, oh God!" Jakob prayed, whether silently or out loud he couldn't tell. He suddenly knew it had to be less than moments before one of his brothers would be dead.

If he wasn't already.

3 · Music to Their Ears

∾

Long pig, sweet meat,
Strong swig, fleet treat,
I don't want to be hung up.
For dinner.

Short tale, long death,
Quart ale, wrong breath,
I don't want to be hung up.
For dinner.

Give me a choice of meat or soy,
Give me a choice of girl or boy,
Give me a choice or give me chance,
A great big meal or a real romance.

Slow boil, quick take,
Low oil, thick steak,
I don't want to be hung up.
For dinner.

Hot ice, cold drink,
Caught twice, old stink,
I don't want to be hung up.
Over dinner.

—Words and music by
Jakob and Erik Griffson,
from *Troll Bridge*

Radio WMSP: 10:00 A.M.

"And now, here's Jim Johnson with our continuing coverage of the 'Disappearing Dairy Darlings.' Jim?"

"Thanks, Katie. After three days, police have still come up empty in their search for the whereabouts of this year's twelve Dairy Princesses. There just seems to be no evidence whatsoever. It's as if the twelve young ladies have fallen off the face of the earth, leaving behind only the butter sculptures of their heads back at the State Fair grounds refrigerators."

"How are their parents holding up, Jim?"

"They've offered rewards of fifty thousand dollars for each girl. And . . ."

"Hold on, Jim—we are being interrupted by Brian Gustafson and a news bulletin."

"Thanks, Katie. Brian Gustafson here, live from Vanderby. Local police have just fished a car out of the Vanderby

River, a car believed to belong to the popular singing group, The Griffson Brothers. A black sedan with vanity plates reading, 'LUV U.' "

"Like their hit song?"

"Exactly, Katie. Apparently, the car lost control on the Trollholm Bridge shortly after sundown, crashing onto the rocks you see behind me."

"This is radio, Brian."

"Right. Well, the rocks behind me are jagged granite, a gray blue in color. 'Troll high,' as they say in Vanderby, and just as dangerous."

"Brian, this is Jim Johnson. Is the car still hung up on the rocks?"

"No, Jim, it apparently hit the rocks before sliding into the river. The Griffsons' parents have confirmed that their three boys had taken the car for a drive. Police have brought back the divers and tracking dogs, but no bodies have been found so far."

"Vanderby? The Trollholm Bridge? Is there any connection between this accident and the disappearance of the Dairy Princesses, Brian?"

"No one is commenting on that, Jim. Yet. But it's the second big-name disappearance this week, and the coincidences are starting to pile up. All we know for certain is that our thoughts and prayers are with the parents of the Griffsons as well as the Dairy Princesses this morning, and we hope that they're all found safe and sound before too long."

"And the Sjogren family—the photographer, don't forget. We send our best to them, too. But it doesn't look good, does it, Brian?"

"No, Katie, it doesn't. The police are puzzled and there have been no ransom notes. And that's all I have. This is Brian Gustafson, reporting live from Vanderby, Minnesota."

"Thanks, Brian. [Sighs.] This is so weird, Jim."

"You betcha."

"My daughter loves the Griffson Brothers. She has posters of them on the wall. Especially that Galen. What a cutie."

"My daughters, too. I'm stunned, Katie."

"Oh my gosh, Jim, we'll have to ask the Spinning Sisters to play the Griffsons' music tonight. And we'll all be saying prayers for their safe return."

· 11 ·

Moira

Moira had no idea how long she'd lain in the box, trying to
match her breathing to the slow rhythm of the other girls.
She'd heard Aenmarr enter the cottage, kiss his wife loudly,
exclaim something about princesses, then leave again with
just as much noise.

And then she heard a scuffling and a yawning that sounded
like a pride of lions rising from sleep.

And now she could hear the troll mother, Trigvi, puttering around the cottage.

Stupidly, Moira thought, *Puttering trolls make a lot of noise.*
There were the footsteps like timpani, the cymbal sound of
pots clanging, and . . .

Oh, God, no!

Trigvi had begun a tuneless humming as she prepared to
cook. She sang in no particular key. The random notes sent
shivers up and down Moira's spine.

This is worse than pop music, Moira moaned silently, suppressing an overwhelming need to shudder. She reminded herself that if she succumbed to her urge to leap from the box shouting, "Shut up! Shut up! For the love of all things musical, please stop that awful humming!" well, then, that would be the end of her. *But, oh Lord, it's torture.* The problem was that no one without perfect pitch could understand how awful it felt.

Then she heard something else.

"Hey! Get me down from here!" It was a boy's voice.

Sounds like he's about my age, Moira thought. *And it's sounds like he's shouting from . . .* Moira couldn't help herself. She gulped hard. *The larder.*

The troll woman's humming stopped.

Thank you, God, Moira prayed.

Trigvi called in a voice deep and loud enough to shake the cottage walls, "Buri, be a good boy. Be shutting dinner up. Your father be home soon."

Basso cantante, Moira thought.

"Yes, Mother," came the reply, as low as Trigvi's but more youthful in timbre.

Moira heard footsteps. A door creaking open.

"What are you?" cried the boy. Then there was a thud and the boy spoke no more.

Moira stifled a gasp.

"Thank you," Trigvi told her son. "I be hating it when dinner speaks." Then she began humming again.

No, no, no, no, Moira kept repeating to herself. *They just killed that poor boy. And now they're going to eat him!* Not to leave herself out of the horror she added, *And then I'm going to end up married to the one who's doing the eating.*

Not even Trigvi's humming annoyed her now. Moira was in a panic. It was worse than when she'd been clinging to Aenmarr's back. At least then, she'd been *doing* something.

Moira had never had stage fright, but she'd talked to musicians who'd had it bad, and she tried to remember what they did to fight it. *Stay calm. Concentrate on breathing. Think of something else. Go to your "happy place," somewhere you feel safe.*

Gritting her teeth, Moira lay still in the box, clenched her fists and forced herself to remember the most difficult passages of the new Berlin piece, imagining the fingering she'd have to use. She tried to think of her mother, her father, her friends at school and in the orchestra. She pictured herself in serene, calming places: Lake of the Isles, Minnehaha Falls, Carlson Peak.

Nothing worked. She began to tremble uncontrollably. Sweat formed on her palms, her forehead, pooled under her arms.

Any minute they're going to smell me in here.

That thought did little to calm her.

Oh God, oh God, oh God, she thought, not even a prayer, but a plea. She couldn't breathe, the sweat, the trembling . . . But just before she reached the breaking point, a familiar voice popped into her head.

"Child of man and woman. Did you miss me?"

Foss had returned.

Where have you been? Moira thought at him furiously, suddenly able to breathe again. The trembling eased.

"I have recruited help," Foss answered. "Though they know it not." There was a pause. Then, "Are you ready to move?"

Very. Though she wasn't sure if any of her limbs would actually work.

"Good. I will . . ."

But before she discovered what the fox was going to do, a sharp *yip* sounded from outside the cottage, like a dog—or a fox—in great pain.

Foss? She sat up.

There was no reply.

Foss? Foss!

Then, she heard—like an unholy combination of a speeding locomotive and summer thunder—a peal of roaring laughter.

Aenmarr, she thought, lying back down in the box. *Why is he so happy?*

A door boomed open and Moira heard Aenmarr speak for the first time. *Basso profundo.* "Trigvi! Second wife! It is time for my second supper."

Foss? Answer me! But he was silent.

He said he'd recruited help. But he also said the help didn't know they'd been recruited.

Doomed, she thought. *Doomed to become a troll bride.*

LIKE MANY A PRISONER, MOIRA discovered that it's hard to maintain a state of constant terror. Eventually captivity is boring. Moira's ears became her eyes, and as she lay in the box, she listened carefully to the trolls.

She could hear them getting ready for their meal. And as long as she didn't think about what they were making for dinner, it was astonishing how normal it all began to sound.

Trigvi popped out to the garden. The door slammed after her.

Buri banged a bowl with a stick in no discernible meter, while asking his father a never-ending stream of questions. "Papa, why be the sun turning us to stone? Papa, who be the princesses? Papa, what be Buri eating? Papa, where be Mama Trigvi going?"

Aenmarr sighed and burped and—from the sound of it—scratched portions of his anatomy that Moira didn't dare guess at.

Oddly, it made her miss her own home.

Trigvi returned with vegetables, calling out "Tatoes and carrows! Soooo good, my lovelies."

Buri was set the task of chopping them. "Choppy-whoppies, my good boy," Trigvi told him in her deep voice. He started his chopping task with great glee, which thankfully took all his concentration, forcing him to stop his incessant question-asking. Moira heard a *whoosh* as a fire was lit, then the steady crackling of flames.

With a great wheezing sigh, Aenmarr said, "I be getting ups and going to the larder to sharpen my knives. Tell me when the pot be boiling in the fireplace, wife."

Moira heard him stomp off into the larder, and soon the telltale *swish-swash* of a knife being run across a whetstone came to her. She remembered the huge knives that hung on the larder wall in his first wife's house, on their ironwork lattice, and the ax on the table, atop a suspicious dark stain.

She thought about the boy who'd cried out and had been swatted into silence.

Too frightened now even to tremble, she lay still, a single tear squeezing past her closed eyelids. She couldn't think of anything else to do.

· 12 ·

Jakob

Running flat out in the darkness toward the sound of a blade being honed, knowing he had only seconds until one of his brothers was murdered, Jakob nearly knocked himself silly against the stone of a cottage wall.

"Oof." The breath went out of him as he fell to the ground. *Too late, too late,* he wailed in his head.

Swish-swash, the knife-sharpening went on.

Maybe not too late. He gulped, stood. *I hope.*

Suddenly, he heard a new sound behind him, like the high-pitched whine of an injured animal. Peering into the darkness, he made out a shape moving in his direction. He tried to give no hint that he was there. Closer, closer it came, until he could see that it was the fox, crawling painfully toward him, its two hind legs dragging.

Can't get distracted by that fox, Jacob thought. *Have to get in and rescue my brother.*

Pushing himself to his feet, Jakob eyed the wall that had knocked him down. It was huge. Then he turned to the fox and whispered, "Sorry, fella. Don't have time to help."

The fox growled.

"Draw Aenmarr away." The words popped into Jakob's head unbidden.

Jakob blinked. "I . . ."

"Draw Aenmarr away."

Jakob shook his head—hard this time—and moved back from the wall, giving the fox a wide berth.

Despite its injured legs, the fox leapt up and bit him on the ankle, hard enough to break the skin.

"Ow!" Jakob yipped and tried to jump away, but the fox kept hold of his pants leg, tumbling him to the ground.

"Child of man," came the voice in Jakob's head again. "Your brother has little time. You must draw Aenmarr away." Then the fox let go of his pants. Staring eye to eye with Jakob, the fox nodded.

This is getting crazier and crazier, Jakob thought. "Ummm . . . why?" he asked, not really expecting an answer.

"Because, human child, other help is at hand."

A small sliver of hope piercing his heart, Jakob asked: "What help?"

"Draw Aenmarr away."

"Okay. Okay," Jakob said, letting out a long breath.

"Go."

Jakob stood, stared for a second at the wall. Then he took a few quiet steps to his left, found a corner, and peeked around what seemed to be the front of the cottage. A bit of light leaked around the edges of a door, illuminating its size. The door went up and up and up, too big for him to open.

And what do I do once I get it open anyway? he thought. *Say, "Hi, trolls, dinner is here"?*

"Go!" the fox commanded again. "Your brother needs a hero."

I'm no hero. Trailing his hand against the rough stone of the cottage wall, he marched toward the front door.

The oak door towered above him and Jakob noted an angular-looking P carved into the middle. P *for petrifying,* he thought. P *for powerful.* "Here goes." Reaching up, he made a fist and knocked on the door as hard as he could. P *for pounding.*

Swish . . . The sound of blade-sharpening suddenly stopped.

A young troll voice inside called out, "Papa, who be pounding on the door so early?"

Aenmarr's dreadful voice answered, "Perhaps your younger brother, Oddi. He be missing his meal, so busy playing silly buggers."

"Should I be letting him in, Papa?"

"Let him stew, Buri."

Unfortunate choice of words, Jakob thought, remembering what had happened to poor Oddi. He pounded on the door again.

"Aenmarr!" he called out huskily. It came out a lot squeakier than he'd hoped. "Come out and meet your . . . er . . . doom!"

From inside came thunderous grumbling, then earth-shaking footsteps as Aenmarr bellowed: "Fools! And damned fools besides. I be thinking I be done with fighting knights and heroes. Besides, swords be giving me indigestion. It be why I agreed to the Compact."

The door was flung open and Aenmarr's grotesque head glared out. He belched and said, "Who be daring to disturb my dinner?"

Jakob froze like a prairie dog beneath a circling hawk. But Aenmarr gazed right over him squinting into the darkness. "Fiddle-foddle," he roared. "More silly buggers." Then he slammed the door shut in Jakob's face.

Jakob stood open-mouthed before the enormous door, unable to believe his luck. After a long moment, he turned and said to the darkness, "What now?"

"Draw Aenmarr away."

Jakob sighed, turned back, and hammered on the door once more. "Aenmarr! Your . . . um . . . doom still awaits you." He took a deep breath and added, "Show yourself, you big hairy ape."

"Hairy ape?" the fox's voice in his head asked. "Aenmarr will not know what a hairy ape is."

Jakob shrugged and ran back to the middle of the clearing. When Aenmarr didn't come out immediately, the fox said, "Try again."

Jakob started toward the house when the door swung open and Aenmarr stood there, filling the doorway. This time he looked straight at Jakob.

"You be a small one," Aenmarr said. "For a prince." He smiled. It was not a reassuring smile. He turned his head to hiss something over his shoulder. Jakob couldn't make out what he said.

I have to get him out of the house somehow. "Come, Aenmarr!" Jakob yelled. "Your . . ."

"Yes, yes, my doom be awaiting me and all that fol-de-rol." Aenmarr waved his massive hand dismissively. "Let us be talking a bit first, young prince."

Jakob couldn't believe what he was hearing. The troll wanted to discuss things? With his dinner? He wondered if Aenmarr recognized him. Or did all dinners look alike?

"Okay. Why . . ." Jakob gulped, then remembered how easy it had been to fool Oddi. He knew what to say. "Why don't you come a little closer. I can't really see you from here."

The troll chuckled. It sounded like the throttling rumble of a big motorcycle. "I be quite fine here. Now tell me," the troll said, scratching his belly and then his behind, "in what way be you my doom?"

Something's very wrong here, Jakob thought. *Trolls were supposed to be dumb. But this one just sounded . . . well . . . crafty.* He bit his lip, and wondered how he might be crafty back. Then he had it. "You'll just have to catch me to find out!" he called.

"I be too old and too tired to be running after you, Little Doom," Aenmarr sighed. "You must be coming here to kill me."

What a predicament. Jakob had been running away from trolls all night. And now, when he actually *wanted* one to chase him, the stubborn creature refused. It just didn't make any sense.

"Well?" Aenmarr asked. "Be you coming to me, my Little Doom?"

Any suggestions? Jakob hoped the fox could hear his thoughts.

The reply was immediate. "Yes, human child. Hurry. Aenmarr is the only troll left in the house. I do not know when the others will return."

The only one left? Jakob thought. *I wonder where the . . .*

Just then, he heard something behind him and spun to face whatever it was. A huge shape reared up from the darkness, a long blade clutched in its hand. Jakob leaped backward, almost tripping over his own feet in his hurry to escape. And almost ran right into another, slightly less huge shape coming at him from the other side.

Suddenly, Jakob came to a terrible realization: Trolls weren't entirely stupid. While Aenmarr had been keeping him busy, the troll's wife and child had sneaked out the back door, skinning knives in their hands, to circle around behind Jakob.

"Away, human child!" cried the fox urgently.

But Jakob didn't need any urging. He did a forward roll between the smaller troll's legs.

Wheeesst! came the sound of a knife blade slicing through the air far too close to his back. Then he was up and running, sparing only a single glance over his shoulder.

Aenmarr was already out of the doorway and loping after him, tree trunk legs eating up the ground between them at a horrifying rate, and yelling "Doom! Come back, Doom!"

Jakob paid no attention to the troll, and just kept on running.

· 13 ·

Moira

Foss . . . Foss, Moira called silently. *What's happening?* The house had suddenly become quiet. *Too quiet.* She tried to sit up, to peek over the side of the box, but fear, like an old habit, clamped her limbs and she couldn't move.

"Get up, child of man."

Child of man and woman, Moira answered automatically, wondering if she could sit up now.

"Get up, child of man and woman." The fox's voice had the same tone as her harp teacher when Moira had made the same mistake three times in a row: slightly sharp and slightly tired.

Get up and go where?

"To the larder."

The larder was the last place she wanted to go. She'd never actually seen a dead body. A dead, chopped-up body. She and her parents were vegetarians, for gosh sakes.

"He is not dead, human child. Listen."

Listening was something she was good at. So she lay in the box and listened to the soft, almost imperceptible breaths of the girls in the box with her. To the snap of the fire in the hearth. To a soft pain-filled groan coming from . . . the larder.

"The larder!" Sitting up, Moira whispered, "Foss, he's *not* dead."

"I told you, human child. You must get up quickly and go into the larder and save him."

She got up, stepping over the four girls, who didn't even flutter a lash at her.

"My limbs still work!" She felt as if she hadn't moved in a week. "But . . ." She hesitated. "What about them?" She pointed to the girls who lay as still as dolls. Four here, seven more elsewhere.

"Leave them. I told you, this is only Thor's Day. We have till tomorrow."

"Today would be better than tomorrow." She stretched out her arms, worked her stiff fingers, wondered if she'd ever be able to play the harp again.

"The princesses are under an enchantment. You could not move them by yourself. Help is here."

She gazed speculatively around the room. "Help is where?"

"In the larder."

Oh!

She ran into the larder. In it stood a troll-sized oak table and three troll chairs, two at the ends and a smaller one snugged in on the side closest to the larder door.

A boy about her age with sandy-colored hair hung upside down from the ceiling, a heavy beige rope knotted around his ankles. The far end was tied to an iron hook on the wall. Another rope was wrapped tightly around the boy's body, keeping his arms against his side. He was moaning.

"Stop moaning. The trolls will hear you," she warned.

He stopped moaning and turned his head toward the sound of her voice. The left side of his face was already purpling where the troll must have hit him earlier to shut him up. The right eye was a startling blue. Even in the dim candlelight of the larder she could see that.

"Trolls?" he whispered. "They were *trolls*? Like in fairy tales—trolls?"

"What did you think they were?"

"Huge. But then lots of folk in Minnesota are huge. Viking stock. I thought they were . . . kidnappers. Wanting ransom."

"Ransom?"

He sighed. "You know. For giving me back."

"They don't give back people. They eat people." She said it matter-of-factly.

"Cannibals?" He moaned again. "I thought you said they were trolls. Can you get me out of here?" His voice rose. "Now?"

"Shhh." She came closer, stared up at him. He was hanging about a foot and a half above her.

He stared back. "Are you a troll, too?"

She laughed, a short sharp bark, like the fox. "Do I *look* like a troll?"

He gulped. "You look like a . . ."

"I'm a musician. And . . ."

"Let me guess," he said. "A Dairy Princess."

She gawked at him as, all unaccountably, he broke into song. His voice was a pleasant tenor, and he was on key, the more surprising since he was upside down.

And he was singing:
What's better than a butter girl?
Badder than my better girl.
Best when I'm not buttered up as well . . .

He began coughing so strongly, he bounced up and down on the rope.

"I'm going to try to get you down," she told him, keeping her voice low and sensible.

He stopped coughing. Closed his good eye and opened it again. "Ready when you are. Just do it."

She spotted six wooden-handled knives hanging from pegs on the whitewashed wall. Each knife looked as large as a sword. Two had serrated edges and one had a hammer-like thing on the bottom of the handle. But they were far too high up for her to reach.

Then she noticed a honing strap and a seventh knife on a three-legged chopping block by the side of the dining table. The chopping block was also above her head, but she thought she might be able to push it over if she could get a good run at it. Three legs were not as steady as four.

"Hold on," she told the boy.

"Is that a joke?"

She ignored him and, backing up till she felt the far wall behind her, she pushed off. Hands straight ahead of her, she ran full tilt at the nearest leg of the chopping block.

Striking it hard, she got it teetering. Quickly, she gave a half turn and shoved her shoulder into the front legs and the stocky chopping block fell over, clattering onto the floor.

"So much for being quiet," he called down to her.

Her shoulder hurt. "Best I could do," she muttered, and picked up the knife that was as big as a broadsword. All the while she was thinking, *Stupid, ungrateful boy,* quickly followed by, *Shut up, Moira.* Because of course he was scared and saying the first thing that came to mind. At least he'd stopped moaning.

Foss' voice came sharply into her head. "What was that unholy racket?"

"Hero at work," she shot back at him. "Why aren't you in here helping?"

"Who are you talking to?" the boy asked.

"Foss." As if that told him anything.

"Who is he? Another troll?"

"He's . . . he's another musician," she said.

"That makes three of us," the boy said.

But if he's a musician, too, Moira wondered, *why doesn't he hear Foss?*

The fox didn't answer, nor did she expect him to. He was very good at giving orders and being tricky. But when it came to the actual hard work, he was never around.

Lugging the heavy knife back to the hanging boy, Moira swung it with all her might at the rope attached to the iron hook.

The knife bounced off, making no impression on the rope. None at all.

"Well," Moira said, huffing with effort, "that was fun." Her arms ached from the blow.

"Saw . . ." the boy said to her, his voice a raspy whisper. "Use it like a saw."

He was right, and she immediately began sawing at the rope, the heavy knife held high over her head. It was a very uncomfortable position but, she supposed, comfort was hardly something heroes ever worried about. "This is a very tough rope," she told him, "so I'll have to do it strand by strand."

She sawed until she thought her arms would fall off her shoulder. Back and forth, back and forth. Suddenly the strand parted with a loud *pop*!

"There . . . that's the first one. Now for the second." The rope was braided, which made it extra strong. Good for hanging up dinner. Bad for cutting through. It took some time.

"A third . . ."

"Just let me know when it's all gone through," he interrupted, "so I'll be expecting the fall."

"Okay."

"I need to be prepared. I was a Boy Scout, you know. Not for very long. Hated the uniform."

He was babbling now. *Just as well*, Moira thought. *It will keep his mind off the trolls.* She sawed through a fourth strand, without answering him back. Then a fifth.

"Child of man, the trolls . . ." came Foss's voice.

"And woman," Moira whispered, as the last strand began to part.

"Last one," she said, to alert the boy, before placing the knife on the floor so as to be ready to help him.

But this strand didn't burst apart as the others had. Rather it unraveled, slow enough that she had time to catch him as he fell. They both went over backward, though she managed to cradle him against her body. It turned out he couldn't stand up on his own.

She scrambled out from under him and pulled him to his feet.

"Cut them. Cut the ropes. . . ."

"How about saying thanks?" she asked huffily.

"Hurry, child of . . ." Foss began.

"Oh shut up," Moira cut him off. "We're almost out of here!"

"I don't want to shut up," the boy said.

"Not you—Foss." But explaining would take too much time. "Trolls coming," she said. "Not going to cut the rest of the ropes here." She grabbed up the heavy knife and pushed the boy out the back door ahead of her.

He didn't argue, just stumbled out soundlessly.

Jakob

Jakob raced headlong into the gloom, the thunderous footsteps of the pursuing trolls spurring him on.

"Doom!" Aenmarr laughed as if it were all just a game.
"Why be you running? It only toughens the meat."

Desperately, Jakob ran on.

There was no moon in Trollholm, but Jakob's eyes were
now fully adjusted to the dark. To his left, patches of lumi-
nescent moss clung to pale, sketchy birches. On his right, an
odiferous fog rose, green and glowing from a nearby swamp.
Will-o'-the-wisps, like demented, oversized fireflies, darted
all around.

Jakob kept sprinting over the uneven ground.

"Doom, Doom, Doom," Aenmarr chanted in time with
his footsteps. A big bass drum of a voice.

He sounds closer, Jakob thought, pushing himself to go
faster. His breath came out in rasping, wheezing gasps. But

he was already running as fast as he could. The trolls' huge legs carried them along with much greater speed. He thought: *What can I do? Put on a sudden growth spurt?*

"Doom, Doom, Doom, you be making a lovely dinner," called Aenmarr's wife.

"Doom, Doom, Doom," added Aenmarr's son. "I be glad you are not thinner."

Aenmarr roared with laughter. "That be it my lovelies! What else?"

"Doom, Doom, Doom, do not run away in fright!"

"Doom, Doom, Doom, come dine with us tonight!"

The three trolls hooted and howled, but Jakob's stomach flipped over. He couldn't outrun them; he'd have to find somewhere to hide. There was that swamp, but he didn't want to escape the trolls just to drown in some sinkhole.

Has to be the forest, he thought, angling left toward a strange awkward stand of trees. *Maybe I can find a stick to fight them off with.* This thought did little to cheer him. It would have to be a very big stick. Tree-sized.

He imagined he could feel the trolls' hot breath on his back as they continued to chant behind him.

"Doom! Doom! Doom!"

Brambly branches slapped him in the face. Tree roots seemed to reach up and coil around his ankles. *Seem to?* he thought, now in full panic. *In this forest, maybe they actually can!*

Pressing deeper into the woods, he dodged bushes and trees, sidestepped rocks and fallen limbs, leapt over a narrow stream, twisted his ankle, stumbled, recovered . . . and ran smack into the thick trunk of an old oak. His vision went white, and the breath flew out of him in a painful rush.

I'm dead, he thought as he fell back onto the mossy ground, lying there trying to get his breath back. *The trolls will come crashing in here any second.*

Staggering to his feet, Jakob began running again. His head swam and he collapsed once more. Crawling to a tree, hoping to hide, he was suddenly struck with the silence around him. The drum of footsteps behind him had stopped. So had the chanting. Jakob lay still, listening, trying to figure out what was going on. Or not going on.

Just then he heard a strange *whoosh*ing accompanied by a crackle of branches. He threw himself sideways and it was lucky he did, because at that very moment an uprooted tree came crashing through the canopy of the forest, landing where he'd been lying just seconds before. A gout of dirt and dead leaves sprayed over him.

"Did you hit him, Papa?"

"No." Jakob heard Aenmarr sigh. "Luck of the very Devil our Little Doom has."

Desperately, Jakob started crawling again, listening intently for another flying tree, or for the booming footsteps to start up again.

There was nothing.

Why aren't they chasing me?

Slowly it came to him: Moving through the forest was easier for him than for the trolls. He could squeeze between the trees; the bigger trolls had to go around, or stomp through, or simply—as Aenmarr had—pull the trees from the ground and toss them.

This realization gave Jakob strength and he pushed himself to his feet. He'd found his way into the trees by accident—but it might be the one bit of terrain in this awful place where he could outpace the trolls.

"Come, my lovelies," Aenmarr said. "This chase be boring me. I be too hungry to continue. After dinner, I be sniffing Doom out. He not be getting far. He bleeds."

I do? Jakob put his hand to his face where he could still feel the sting from the branches. It came away wet. *I guess I do.*

"There be no place in Trollholm he can hide from Aenmarr for long." The trolls' footsteps started up again, but receding this time.

Jakob sighed gratefully and staggered in the opposite direction, wondering if he had done anything more than buy himself a few hours. And wondering as well if any of his running and bleeding and terror had helped save either of his brothers.

JAKOB WALKED FOR WHAT FELT like hours, through what seemed to be the same thick dark. Suddenly, he stumbled upon a stream at the far edge of the woods. Barely a trickle really. He followed it, thinking it should bring him eventually to the river, and from there—maybe—home. He no longer believed he could help his brothers by fighting the trolls, or by leading the trolls away. He doubted he could help the fox, for that matter. All he could think of was to get as far from the trolls as possible.

He walked beside the stream and, every few steps, bent down to splash cold water onto his face to stop the small cuts from bleeding. When the brush got too thick for him to keep the stream in sight, he followed it by the sound of its burbling.

A little farther on, the dark now more of a deep gray, he found a muddy game trail—*Hopefully a herbivore,* he thought. He recognized the trail from the once-a-year hunting trips his father and uncles took them on. Griffson Greenhorns they called themselves. Galen was especially good at it. Jakob had never been keen on hunting. Who would have thought those three-day adventures might one day come in handy for escaping a pack of murderous trolls.

For that matter, who would ever have thought of murderous trolls?

But thinking back on those hunting trips brought tears to Jakob's eyes. The Griffsons would never again be able to . . .

He gave a quick swipe to his eyes with his sleeve. No time to get misty. He had to be strong. Someone needed to alert the police to what was going on here.

Trotting down the game trail, he found the stream again. Here it widened, now five feet across, with smooth rocks jutting out of the flowing water like stepping stones. Jakob didn't think the water was deep, but just in case, he hopped from rock to rock instead of wading. It was certainly easier going that way than pushing through the thick undergrowth.

AFTER LONG MINUTES OF TRAVELING over the stepping stones—it was light enough now to see that much—Jakob decided he could no longer call the flowing water a stream. It was now a full river, wide and swift, the stones too far apart for safe jumping. He made his way to a rocky shingle that jutted out from the right hand bank and continued on.

The sound of the water put him in mind of a new song. He began humming it to himself, his fingers idly forming the chords to back the melody.

I wish I had my guitar, he thought. *This is a real good one. Could call it "Walking River" or something.* An opening line sprang into his head. *"I'm not gonna die on the river . . ."*

Suddenly, he realized that this was the first time he'd thought of music since being captured by Aenmarr. *I wonder if it's this place, or that before I had enough to think about, just trying to stay alive.*

He didn't ponder long, but let the new melody take him. Matching his steps to the beat, he hummed the tune, hearing the guitar accompaniment in his head. Soon, the timbre of the river changed, flowing faster or deeper or maybe both, Jakob wasn't sure, but he let the melody follow. He imagined a big upright bass leading the guitar into double time and smiled. Whistling, he heard the river start to roar.

"Drums!" he cued his imaginary band, and percussion crashed in his head. It was a full band now, screaming out a strange bluegrass-metal-Celtic tune unlike anything he and his brothers had ever recorded. He was so obsessed with the new song that he didn't recognize what the river's new roar meant.

The ground fell away beneath his feet, and Jakob teetered on the edge of a precipice.

"Holy guacamole!"

A huge open space loomed before him. Windmilling his arms, Jakob tried to regain his balance. He couldn't actually see where the space ended, but he sensed that the ground was a long way down. After a terrifying second or three, he found his equilibrium and threw himself backward, jarring his butt painfully on the rocks.

"Waterfall!"

Now the river's roar made sense, only he'd been too caught up in his music to figure it out. Getting onto his knees, he crawled forward carefully, feeling his way with his hands as much as his eyes, till he found the edge. Then he peered over.

Misty, half-formed cliffs to the left, cliffs to the right, and the river plummeting down into the darkness. He couldn't see any bottom. It was as if the world ended here.

And so will I, Jakob thought miserably.

He didn't dare backtrack too far. He'd end up at one of Aenmarr's houses and in the stew pot. And he couldn't go any farther this way. No wonder Aenmarr wasn't worried about me getting too far. Jakob wanted to scream in frustration.

He didn't, because just then, he heard voices over the roar of the falls. Scooting forward just a touch, he peered into the darkness and his eyes adjusted to the gloom.

There!

Somewhere below him, there *was* a path. Jakob could tell this, because he could just make out some figures moving next to the cliff walls.

The trolls! he thought desperately. *They tricked me again. Made me think they were leaving, then doubled around in front of me.* Though he couldn't think how they could have done that unless Trollholm was built on some kind of circle or plate, which didn't make any sense at all.

He started to scrabble backward, to hide, for there was light now, rising swiftly in front of the figures. Daylight coming up with the force of an oncoming storm. Then he froze in a panic, because when he'd moved, he'd sent a shower of small stones down the cliff face, pattering right behind the figures below. As he watched in horror, they turned and looked up.

And saw him.

· 15 ·

Moira

The boy went out the back door and hesitated. Moira shoved him with two fingers.

"Left," she whispered.

He turned, went as far as the wall's end, hesitated again and glanced back at her. Still bound up in the rope, he looked incredibly vulnerable.

Moira hauled the larder door closed, or as closed as she could without being able to reach the handle. Then she moved past the boy and peered cautiously around the corner. A small bundle of fur lay against the far end of the wall, near the next corner, like a discarded rag.

"Foss?" she hissed.

"Be silent, human child. The trolls come home."

"Which way?" she asked in her head.

"Front door."

"Ah!" She grabbed the boy by the shoulder, propelling him forward.

"Who are you talking to?" he asked. "I hear a kind of buzz, but . . ."

She clapped a hand over his mouth, all the while thinking: *So he can sort of hear Foss.* Then she realized what this meant. *This place is lousy with musicians.*

"As long as they are not lousy musicians," Foss said in their heads. If a fox can be said to chuckle, he chuckled. "This one is just passable. He will get used to me."

Quickly, they made their way to him.

"Lying down on the job?" Moira asked sharply. Then she realized that his hind feet were splayed out behind him in an unnatural position. "That doesn't look very good." She knelt down.

"You may touch me this time, child of man and woman, but remember—I am no pet."

She nodded, then stood and spun the boy around. Taking the sword-like knife, she made quick work of the rope that bound him. When she was done, and the rope in pieces at his feet, he shook his hands vigorously to get the circulation back. His face showed nothing of what must have been a horrible case of pins-and-needles. Moira was impressed, but didn't say so.

"You carry this," she said, handing him the knife. "I'll take the fox." She bent down again and gathered Foss up in her arms. Just then she heard the front door of the troll's house slam shut.

"My fiddle," Foss said sharply.

"Never mind the stupid fiddle."

"Without the fiddle, we cannot rescue the eleven princesses."

"Why?" she asked.

"Trust me."

"Hey!" said the boy suddenly. "I hear a voice in my head!"

"Shhh!" Moira and Foss said together. Then Moira bent down and grabbed up the fiddle with her right hand, careful not to jar the wounded fox. "It's the fox," she whispered.

"Really? No." He was careful to whisper back. Glancing quickly down at the fox in her arms, he looked up again, quizzically. "Really?"

Moira shrugged and said quietly, "Why would I make such a thing up?" Then to Foss, "Which way?"

"The path to the right. It leads below the waterfall and back to my cave. We will be safe there, child of man . . . and woman."

Just then Moira heard bellowing in the house, and guessed the trolls weren't happy about their loss of dinner. She asked no more questions but raced away down the right-hand path, the boy following quickly.

"Hurry, hurry," she whispered over her shoulder to the boy, who carried the knife on his left shoulder like a sword. *Stupid boy*, she thought. *Show off.*

He caught up to her, shifted the sword to his right shoulder, and held his hand out for the fiddle.

Wordlessly, she gave it to him.

He grinned at her. Even with the one closed eye and the bruise along the side of his face, he was good-looking.

And knows it, she thought. The last thing she wanted to do was get a crush on a musician. Especially one who was likely to be a troll dinner before the night was out.

The fox continued to give them instructions, though his sendings were laced with grunts of pain. "Here!" he said. "Turn here."

They turned.

"Watch out for the tree branch across the path."

The boy ducked under it, and Moira followed, thinking, *A troll could step right over that.*

Foss continued his instructions to them as they walked along, reminding Moira of her driving teacher. "Watch out—slippery place." And, "Deep hole." And, "Take care. The path goes down sharply and is full of loose pebbles."

They were careful, but not quite careful enough, slipping and sliding at the top of the path, scattering pebbles as they went. Moira was terrified that the trolls would hear them.

Chuckling, Foss said, "Do not worry. We are safe for to-day, human children."

They had gotten to the bottom of the path, which ran by a great roaring waterfall. Moira assumed Foss meant that, with such a noise, the sound of a few pebbles would alert no one. Not even trolls.

"Look—the sun rises," Foss said. "No troll goes out in the sun."

In fact, the sun rose before them as a bright orange disc with such quickness and brilliance, it looked like a bad stage production. Moira was temporarily blinded and heard rather than saw, the pattering of stones around her.

Moira knew it couldn't be the boy. He was ahead of her,

not behind. She was carrying the fox. Fear leapt like a fire in her throat.

"Trolls!" she cried aloud, turning and trying to see up to where the stones were falling from the top of the waterfall. But her eyes were still blasted by the sun.

"Cannot be," said Foss.

"Look!" Moira said, for now she could see again, and she pointed.

Someone knelt at the top of the falls, the sun lighting his horrified face, his long blond hair.

In front of her the boy laughed. "Jakob! Jakob!" he cried out, heedless of any noise. "You're alive." And then his laughter turned to sobs that were loud enough to alert any trolls still out in the neighborhood.

IT TOOK THE BOY JAKOB no more than a minute or two to scramble down the cliff, though at the last he fell into the water and stood up, dripping but triumphant. Wading through the river, he made it to the shore.

"Erik!" he cried. "Oh God, I thought you were stew for sure."

Erik put down both fiddle and knife and raced over to him, hauling him onto the riverbank, where they hugged.

"Look at your face!" Jakob said.

"Look at your clothes," Erik answered.

Moira stared at them both. They had different color hair, but their eyes were the same: widely set apart, and a surprising light blue. Their noses were both small and covered with freckles. And the way they twined their arms around one another, spoke of more than friendship.

"Brothers?" she asked Foss, looking down into his dark, shining eyes.

"It seems so, human child."

∞

WITH FOSS CRADLED IN HER arms, Moira led the way back to the cave. Erik carried the fiddle and Jakob the knife. Moira showed them how to crawl in and when to stand. Then she set the fox down on a bed of dried grass. Turning to the boys, she said to the new boy, "So you are Jakob." To the one she'd rescued, "and you Erik." There'd been no time for introductions before.

They nodded.

"My name is Moira Darr. And this," she pointed at the fox, "is Foss."

"I am the *Fossegrim*," he corrected her.

"Whatever."

"I've met him," Jakob said.

"We're the Griffson Brothers," Erik said. "Well, two thirds anyway." He seemed to be waiting for something, some kind of recognition.

Moira smiled noncommittally. "Okay, Erik and Jakob Griffson," she said, "I have eleven friends in there who need rescuing, or else tomorrow they become trolls' brides."

Jakob took a deep breath. "Our brother Galen is in the larder of Aenmarr's first wife's house. I think he trumps the brides."

"Eleven are more important than one," Moira said.

"But only the one is going to be killed and eaten," Jakob replied.

Erik held up his hands as if weighing something and added, "Marriage, stew, marriage, stew."

"Have you taken a good look at those trolls?" Moira said with an exaggerated shiver. But she knew Jakob was right. Death *was* more worrisome than marriage, no matter how gruesome the groom.

"Be silent human children," the fox told them from his bed of grass. "You argue like trolls. We must count the boy Galen lost. Aenmarr is a stupid beast, driven only by hunger."

"No!" said Jakob and Erik as one.

"We won't give him up like that," Erik added. "Just on your say so." Then he burst into tears that he scrubbed away angrily with a dirty sleeve.

But the fox was relentless. "Why do you think Aenmarr abandoned his chase? Why did he not return to it?" Foss snapped his jaws loudly, as if chewing.

"Shut up!" Erik roared. He leapt at Foss, fists clenched and teeth bared, looking for the moment more animal than the fox.

Jakob caught him, holding him back.

"He's right," Jakob hissed in Erik's ear. "Galen's gone. And there's nothing we can do about it."

"Wise child," Foss said. "Now, listen, else all is lost. All."

They shut up. And listened.

· 16 ·

Jakob

Jakob tried to put Galen out of his mind by listening to what Foss was telling them, but he was having a hard time of it. He kept picturing Oddi's severed head, only this time it was Galen's, his handsome face gazing blankly back. Then Jakob realized suddenly that the fox was staring at him expectantly. The others, too.

"What?"

"I asked," the fox repeated, "if you were listening at all."

Jakob nodded.

"Then what have I been telling you?" Foss sounded just like Jakob's father on a bad day.

"Um . . ." Jakob struggled to remember. Foss had said something about new lands and old gods, dragon boats and ocean voyages. It all seemed kind of remote to what they were dealing with at the moment—death, cannibalism, and forced marriages. He gulped and guessed. "The Vikings? Something about the Vikings?"

Foss yipped. "Something about the Vikings!"

Jakob hadn't realized telepathic thoughts could sound so sarcastic.

"Human child, I am speaking of the birth of Aenmarr. The origin of our enemy! Know your foe and you know how to defeat him."

"Okay, okay," Jakob said. "I'm listening." Though he had to wonder about the wisdom of that since Foss, who professed to know all about Aenmarr, hadn't yet managed to defeat him.

The fox didn't respond to the thought, but simply repeated, "As I was saying, when the first dragon boats crossed the northern ocean and grounded on this new land, they did not come alone. They brought with them their dreams and their nightmares, their old gods and monsters."

"Monsters?" Jakob interrupted, just to show Foss that he was, indeed, listening.

Foss nodded and continued, "Aenmarr is one of those monsters, an ancient troll who sprang to life in the minds of men far from their homeland. His was a familiar terror, almost comforting in that familiarity; something to explain to the newcomers the mysterious slaughtering of livestock, the often bizarre disappearances of their wives and children."

Erik looked puzzled. "But what help is this to us?"

Moira raised her hand, as if she were in class. "He already told us that—to know our enemy. The better question is to ask how come he has all this knowledge."

Show off, Jakob thought.

"The girl is right. Understanding your enemy is halfway to defeating him." Foss shrugged his front shoulders, then winced in pain. "And I have this knowledge, human children," Foss said, "because it is my origin as well."

"You came over on a dragon boat?" Erik asked.

"In a manner of speaking."

This time Jakob couldn't keep silent, but leaned toward the fox and spoke softly. "Were you a god or a monster?"

Foss grinned sharp teeth at him. "A little of both."

Jakob thought grimly, *And why don't I find that comforting?*

The fox licked his lips before continuing. "Now, Aenmarr hunted the settlers, as he had in the old country. And they fought back, just as they always had. But this was a new land, wilder, untamed. There were new enemies whose knowledge of the land was unsurpassed. Neither settlers nor troll could afford to continue with their old enmities and hope to survive."

"I suppose the new enemies were the Native Americans," Moira said. "But who did Aenmarr fight with?"

"The natives had their own gods, human child," replied Foss. "And their own monsters: Unktehi and the Thunderbird, manitous and animal spirits. They resented Aenmarr's intrusion. He battled them constantly."

"So they made a deal?" Moira asked. "Aenmarr and the settlers?"

"Precisely." The fox grinned again, his teeth white and sharp, and nodded his head.

Why didn't I think of that? Jakob thought, this time grudgingly admiring her quickness.

"Wait a minute," Erik said, "what kind of a deal?"

Jakob and Moira looked at one another, eyes wide, then answered him together, "Dairy Princesses!"

"Close," the fox told them, his tone one that a proud teacher uses with his best students. "Instead of wasting their energies fighting each other, they forged a compact. Each year, the settlers would deliver twelve maidens for Aenmarr to consume."

"What?" Erik rose to his knees.

Foss blinked at the interruption, licked his lips, then resumed as if Erik hadn't spoken or moved "In return, he left the settlers alone the rest of the year. Everybody seemed happy with the arrangement."

"Everybody except the girls," corrected Moira. Then with rising indignation, she added, "Are none of you bothered by this? That's . . . that's—"

"Shocking?" Foss said.

Moira shook her head, then found the word she was looking for. "Reprehensible."

"Human child," the fox said, his tone soft but his eyes still glittering, "those were barbarous times, and both parties were struggling for their lives. Besides, the tradition of live maidens did not last long."

"It didn't?" Moira's voice was full of relief.

Foss started to explain, but Jakob spoke first. "The butter heads."

Foss looked pleased.

"You said trolls are hungry creatures," Jakob said. "Give them something that looks just like the maidens they were promised. . . ."

"And that tastes just as good," Erik added. "Aenmarr probably never knew the difference."

"Or perhaps, he just did not care," Foss said. He gave his right paw a quick lick. "It matters not now. For neither maidens nor butter were delivered this year, and the Compact has been broken. Aenmarr has collected what was promised."

"So what can *we* do?" Jakob asked.

The fox's answer was immediate. "Kill Aenmarr."

"All right!" Erik shouted, but Jakob shook his head vigorously.

"No. No killing."

"What's wrong with you, Jakob?" Erik asked. "That monster's killed Galen."

"You wouldn't understand," Jakob said, looking down at his hands. "You've never killed anyone."

"And I suppose you have?" Erik's said sarcastically.

Jakob bit his lower lip.

"Who?"

"Oddi . . ." Jakob whispered.

Erik looked questioningly at Moira who shrugged her shoulders. He appealed to the fox.

"One of Aenmarr's sons," Foss said. "The youngest."

"Wow, little brother." Erik made a fist. "All right!" He cocked his head to one side. "How . . . ?"

"Well, not exactly with my own hands. But it's my fault he died. I saw it. And he didn't deserve . . ." His eyes were suddenly full of tears.

"And Galen did deserve it?"

"Or Mr. Sjogren?" asked Moira.

"Who?" Both boys spoke as one, their voices eerily similar.

"The photographer."

"No, no, no," Jakob said, holding up his hands. "None of them *deserved* to die. But I don't want more deaths. It doesn't solve anything. There must be some other way." He looked at the fox. "Can't we make *another* pact?"

"I doubt Aenmarr is in the mood to negotiate," Foss said. "Besides, he does not want to eat these princesses. He wants them to marry his sons."

"We have to try something," Jakob said.

"After what he's done to Galen?" Erik was furious.

Moira looked at Jakob curiously, waiting for his answer.

Yowling once in amusement, Foss said, "All right, Little Doom, I have been trapped here for centuries without managing to find a way to escape. I am willing to try someone else's idea. As long as my freedom is part of your new Compact, I will assist you. Though I see little hope of your success."

"Thank you." Jakob smiled at the fox, though it was more a grimace than a grin.

"But if your negotiation fails, we must kill Aenmarr. Kill all of them." The fox's voice in their heads was insistent.

"Yeah," breathed Erik. "All of them. Women and children first, if we have to."

Moira raised her hand again. "How do we kill a troll, anyway?"

Foss chuckled mirthlessly. "Not easily. They are big, as you have seen. And more muscle than meat. But they can be beguiled by music, kept at bay by fire, turned to stone by the sun."

Jakob silently mouthed the words *music, fire, sun* over and over, like a mantra, like the beginning of a song.

"But let us drown that kit when we get to it," Foss said. "First, Little Doom is going to talk us out of here." He settled his head on his forepaws, ears twitching back and forth. "Come, child of man, tell us your plan. Then we will sleep a touch till full daylight can set your plan in motion."

Erik and Moira both looked at Jakob expectantly.

Jakob thought: *A plan? What makes him think I have a plan? I don't even have an idea. An inkling. A . . .*

Just then a tiny spark of an idea flared to life in his mind. *Not much of an idea actually. And it probably won't work anyway,* But he had to get them all out of Trollholm without killing anyone else. Or at least he had to try.

4 · Return of Doom

∞

Doom, Doom, Doom
Come back.
In my wee room
I'll hack and whack.

I'll cleft your skull,
And split your skin,
From crotch to jowl,
From toes to chin.

And then I'll make
A tasty stew,
And in I'll take
The rest of you.

Doom, Doom, Doom,
Doom, Doom, Doom.

—Words and music by
Jakob and Erik Griffson,
from *Troll Bridge*

Radio WMSP: 10:00 A.M.

"So, Jim, is there any more news on the missing kids, the Princesses and those princes of pop music, The Griffson Brothers?"

"No, Katie, the police are absolutely at a dead end. No one saw anything. The girls' cars were undisturbed, but the boys' car was destroyed, as if it had been taken up and thrown over the bridge, but the bridge was not touched at all."

"That's the bridge where the butter heads are usually left?"

"Yes, Katie, but as you know, not this year."

"Because of the new mayor."

"Yes."

"And has anyone questioned him, Jim?"

"Glad you asked, Katie. I've just come from a press conference with him. After it was over, I asked him some specific questions."

"Can we hear any of it, Jim?"

"Yah, you betcha, Katie."

<click>

"*Mr. McGuigan, Jim Johnson of Radio WMSP, hoping to ask you a few questions.*"

"*Make it three and I'll do what I can to answer them.*"

"*Do you think there's any connection between the missing kids and the butter heads?*"

"*Don't be silly, Johnson. Why on earth do you think there's a connection?*"

"*Well, because it's the same bridge—*"

"*Ask me your second question. I hope it's better than the first.*"

"*Do you know the history of the butter heads, sir?*"

"*Yes, of course. What kind of mayor would I be if I didn't know? It has to do with old, outmoded superstitions, something any modern American would be embarrassed to cling to. And those heads melting on the bridge were powerfully toxic to the river that, as you know, empties over one of the loveliest waterfalls in the state and into the best damned fishing lake in the Midwest. We folks of Vanderby are proud of that lake. I am a strong environmentalist, as you know. Minnesota is the land of ten thousand lakes and if we do not keep our water pure, we are no better than those superstitious ancestors of ours who believed in monster bogeymen and pacts with the devil and dumped their household waste into the runoff.*"

"*Then, sir, for my third question: What do you think happened to the girls and the Griffsons. And to Mr. Sjogren?*"

"*Haven't you heard about terrorism, man?*"

"*In Vanderby?*"

<click>

"*Do you believe his terrorist theory, John?*"

"*No more than he believes in bogeymen, Katie.*"

"*Thanks, Jim—and now here's Bob with sports.*"

17

Jakob

Jakob was dreaming a song that began: "Music, fire, fire and sun, one life is ended, one life begun—" when he woke abruptly.

"Ouch!" he cried. "Stop that!" Foss was nipping at his sore ankle.

"Up, child of man," ordered the fox.

Jakob groaned.

"Up if you want to set your plan in motion before night-fall."

Jakob sat up and rubbed his eyes. He wanted nothing more than to collapse onto the cave floor and go back to sleep. He'd barely finished sharing his plan—*if you could dignify it with that name*—before falling swiftly into an exhausted slumber. The last thing he remembered was Foss huddled in a corner with Erik, presumably deep in telepathic conversation.

No time for resting, he told himself. Foss was right. They had preparations to make. Fires to set up. Trolls to fool. Compacts to swear to.

He shook Erik by the arm.

"Get off," Erik grumbled sleepily. Then he mumbled, "We late for a gig?"

"Biggest gig of our lives," Jakob told him.

For a moment Erik looked befuddled. Then—glancing around the cave—he pushed himself up on one elbow. "Right, little bro. I remember. Trolls, monsters, cannibals. Let's get moving on this plan of yours." He rolled his shoulders, and put a hand to his bruised face. "Wow, am I sore."

Jakob refused to compare aches and pains. Instead he crawled to the back of the cave to wake up the girl.

"YOU SURE THIS IS GOING to work, Foss?" Jakob was standing at the wood's edge, staring across the meadow. They'd been gathering fuel for the bonfire. "Sure we'll be safe?"

"No," the fox replied. "Nothing is safe around trolls. But trolls fear fire. If you build your ring of flames high enough, then you should be safe enough inside." His toothy grin wasn't reassuring.

"*We* should be?" asked Jakob. "Where are *you* going to be, Mr. Faithful Fox?"

The fox snarled. "This is your plan, Little Doom. And foxes don't do fire any more than trolls. I'll be waiting and watching from here."

"Well, that's just . . ." Jakob began, his voice rising and

breaking. Moira and Erik stared at him expectantly. Jakob took a big breath and started again. "Actually, Foss, you're right. It *is* my plan."

The fox tipped his head to one side, waiting.

"And there's no reason you guys should risk your lives for it." Erik's eyes narrowed. Moira's face was unreadable. "I mean it. Help me get the fire circle set up, and then I'll take it from there."

Foss said nothing, but Erik peered over his armload of dry sticks. "I don't want to lose another brother."

Jakob smiled wanly. "Trust me, I don't want you to lose another one, either. But if I mess up and die, someone will need to kill the trolls and rescue the girls."

Head to one side, Erik said slowly, "Kill the trolls and rescue the girls. There's a song there somewhere."

"And we'll write it when this is over," Jakob promised.

Erik eyed Jakob for another moment. Then, after a brief glance at Foss, he nodded. "All right."

Jakob looked at Moira.

"No," she stated flatly, and went on gathering firewood.

"Um . . . no?" Jakob said.

"That's right, no." Arms now full of wood, Moira marched into the small clearing by the cottages, Jakob and his brother following close behind. She dropped her load onto the steadily-increasing circle of tinder. Pushing a stray lock of hair from her face, she pointed back at Foss with a stiff forefinger. "He's a coward," she said. She jabbed her finger at Erik. "And you're a fool."

"'A fool'?" Erik laughed. "No one under the age of eighty says that."

"Anyone who reads more than a comic book or three does."
Then she glared at Jakob. "And you . . . well . . ." She took a
deep breath. "Well, boys are stupid." She sniffed, and her lips
made a thin line. "How do you think you'll manage the fires
on your own while you're bargaining with Aenmarr? How will
you keep the music going? You'll need someone to help tend
the fire and the song, keep them going all night long. Or you'll
get yourself eaten. See—stupid!" She turned and stomped
back into the forest for another armload of wood.

Open-mouthed, Jakob and Erik watched her march away,
Erik recovered first. Winking at his brother, he said, "She's
feisty. I like that."

Inexplicably, Jakob found himself blushing. "Let's get
the circle finished," he said, changing the subject. "Night's
coming."

LONG SHADOWS, AS FLAT AS black paint, stretched over the circular pile of wood and kindling and were heading toward
the cottages, when Foss signaled that it was time.

"See the rune on that door?" he said, lifting his snout toward the rightmost troll house.

Jakob could just make out the door in the fading light. In
the middle was a carved letter that looked like a *P*, the top
shaped more like a triangle.

"That rune is Wunjo," Foss told him. "It means *joy* and
comfort and *pleasure* and *prosperity*."

"It'll mean *destruction* by the time we're through," muttered Jakob.

The fox departed without another word, and Erik glanced after him before jogging over to Jakob and crushing him in a tight hug.

"You sure this will work?" he whispered. "Because . . ."

Jakob tilted his head back to look up at his older brother. "Because what?" Erik just shook his head, and Jakob patted him on the back. "I taught Galen; I can teach anybody."

Erik frowned. "All right, but if anything goes wrong . . ."

"Nothing will go wrong."

Shaking his head, Erik said. "No, that's not what I mean. It's just . . ." He struggled for words, which was unlike him.

"Just what?" Jakob asked.

Erik pushed Jakob away. "Never mind. Just be careful." He offered up one more tidbit over his shoulder before leaving. "Remember that we're all trying to get out of here as best we can."

"Um . . . okay." Puzzled, Jakob watched his brother sprint off. *Wonder what that was about?* But he didn't wonder for long, because Moira was coming, blazing torches in each hand, and the sun was setting behind the painted forest in a muted display of purples and pinks. Soon all they'd have for light would be the fire.

From inside the nearby cottage, came the rumblings of awakening trolls.

"Fe-fi-fo-fum," Jakob intoned.

Moira giggled. "That's giants," she corrected, putting the torches to the wood.

"And I'm no Jack . . ." Jakob began, but the rest was buried in the crackle of the fire.

18

Moira

As the fire rose higher, so sank the sun. The moment it dropped down behind the mountains, the front door of Trigvi's cottage was flung open.

"Jakob," Moira whispered.

"I see it." He grabbed her hand and gave it a quick squeeze. Then, raising his voice, he began to sing. Except for the first three notes that broke—more with fear, she thought than anything else—he had the most on-key voice she'd heard in a long while. It had a purity and cleanliness that made her catch her breath.

Doom, Doom, Doom
I'm back.
My fiery room
Goes crackle and crack.

I'll tell you true
And I'll not lie,
I'll give to you
A chance to fly.

And then we'll make
Another pact
Or else I'll take
Your living back.

Doom, Doom, Doom,
Doom, Doom, Doom.

A troll boy, a smaller version of Aenmarr, peeked out of the door, his greenish hair spiky and his lower jaw jutting out. He rubbed the sleep from his eyes. "Papa, Papa," he cried, "look—there be fire and Doom."

From within Aenmarr's voice boomed, "You best not be joking with me, my son, Buri. I be just risen and have not eaten yet."

Jakob sang the song again, and Moira joined in, singing a lovely, soaring descant. It gave her courage and heart and hope.

Suddenly Aenmarr appeared in the doorway, towering over his son. His face was thunderous. However, when he realized there was a song coming from within the fire, his face softened slowly. The ugly features, the rough angles took on a kind of innocent longing. "Who . . ." he said, his voice almost purring, "who be making singing here?"

Jakob signaled Moira to keep on singing, then called out, "We do, Aenmarr. Come closer and we will sing it for you."

The troll clomped a stride from his house, then froze. The fire kept him at bay. And as it climbed higher, the flames licking at the tops of the woodpile, Aenmarr stood, mesmerized.

Still, he's too close for comfort, Moira thought. She could see the bile green of his skin, the long sharp fangs. He had a large green wart the size and color of an unripe apple beside his bulbous nose. She skipped a beat in the song out of fear.

Aenmarr growled and flung out his arms.

"Keep on singing," Jacob cried to Moira. "Sing anything you can think of."

Moira segued into "Ave Maria," then the "Star Spangled Banner," and then in a moment of unexplained whimsy, into a nursery song her mother had taught her, about "a troll, fol-de-rol," before coming back to Jakob's "Doom" song.

As she sang, Jakob called out again to the troll, only this time instead of bidding him come closer, he said, "Aenmarr of Trollholm, I am the human Jakob Griffson of Minneapolis here to remake the Compact with you. Will you listen or will I become once more Aenmarr's Doom? For as you have eaten my brother, so I have eaten your son."

Moira gasped, surprised by what he said. She hadn't been expecting it. She stuttered in her song.

But this time Aenmarr didn't notice her mistake. Instead he asked, "Jakob Doom, how be you eating my son?"

"With relish did I eat Oddi, son of Aenmarr, as you ate Galen Griffson."

The troll stepped a foot closer. "Human, you be lying."

Jakob set a few more pieces of wood on the flames while Moira raised her voice and started on three new songs, "Ode to Joy," "Jesu Joy of Man's Desiring," and oddly "Did You Ever See a Lassie?"

The new music stopped the troll. He cocked his massive head and stood listening.

"If I lie," Jakob called out, "where is your son, Oddi, now, Aenmarr of Trollholm? Has his mother seen him lately?"

"Go this way and that . . ." Moira sang. "Go this way and that way. Did you ever see a lassie . . ."

Aenmarr turned back and spoke to the troll boy by his side. "Be running to Mama Botvi's house, Buri, and ask her where her son be sleeping."

"But Papa, I be wanting to see the circle of fire. I be wanting to listen to the . . ."

There was a sharp crack of skin on skin as Aenmarr swatted the troll boy, and then off Buri ran, howling like a hundred hungry gulls squabbling over a scrap of fish.

In little more than three minutes—and three choruses of "This Land Is Your Land" because Moira didn't know the verses—the troll boy was back.

"Papa, Papa," he bawled. "Mama Botvi be saying that Oddi be not home before daylight."

"What say you now, Aenmarr of Trollholm?" called out Jakob. "Shall we talk about that new Compact?" He found some more tree limbs and threw them on the top of the burning wall of fire.

Her voice starting to roughen, Moira segued into the

English version of Humperdink's "Hansel and Gretel" that she'd recently played in a children's concert with the orchestra.

Insane with fury, Aenmarr bellowed and stumbled back into his house. He emerged again brandishing a very large knife, the size of a spear. Moira squeaked as he heaved it at the ring of fire. Luckily it stuck in one of the logs and did not dislodge it.

"Sing louder!" Jakob hissed, then called out again, "Aenmarr of Trollholm, do not anger me, do not call down Doom again."

"Doom, Doom, Doom," sang Moira, remembering half the words of the verses and making up the rest.

"Papa . . ." cried Buri as his mother pulled him into the safety of her house.

Aenmarr threw several more knives, a pot, and three bowls at the ring of fire. One of the bowls managed to sail over the logs and into the center. Still singing, Moira picked it up and wore it as an oversized hat and sang the first verse and chorus of "In My Easter Bonnet."

"Where do you get these songs?" Jakob asked her, awe and amusement warring on his face. Aenmarr was still fuming and strode back into the house for a few more pots giving Jakob more time to add on to the burning wood.

She sang back, "Just trying to keep the music going." Which was no answer. But then she hadn't a clue. She just sang whatever popped into her head, grateful for each and every song.

At last, as Aenmarr's three wives gathered behind him, their voices squabbling, urging him to do something, Jakob called out, "I will not ask again, Aenmarr of Trollholm. I will gather the Dairy Princesses once the sun rises again. They will greet their sister here, the Dairy Queen."

Moira snorted.

"Sing!" he hissed at her.

She winked, then sang:

Doom, Doom, Doom
I'm back.
My fiery room
Goes crackle and crack.

The Dairy Queen,
Who wears the crown,
Can be real mean
And wear you down,

So make a deal
Another pact
Or you will feel
Your sons hijacked.

Doom, Doom, Doom,
Doom, Doom, Doom.

"Impressive," Jakob conceded. "You can write songs for the Griffsons any time you wish."

"Oh. Are you and your brothers in a band?"

Speechless, Jakob stared at her as if she were crazy.

Moira shrugged and launched with gusto into the "Hallelujah Chorus." Her voice was getting hoarse but at least she could still hit the notes. And of course she was right on pitch.

Aenmarr grimaced and held out his hands, either in thrall or in pain, it was hard to tell.

"Tell me what Compact you be wishing, human Doom," cried Aenmarr in submission.

"You turn over the princesses to me and I will teach you to play the guitar," Jakob said.

Aenmarr's hands raked his green-black hair. He roared, "What be a . . . guitar?"

"The fiddle that hangs on the wall of Oddi's house," Jakob said. "Bring it here and I shall show you what I know and what I can teach."

Aenmarr clumped back to the near house. "Buri, be going to Botvi's house and bringing me the fiddle that hangs on the wall. Mind, if you be breaking it, I be breaking your head and boiling its contents into soup." There was another *thwack*ing sound, a cry from the boy, and the sound of pounding feet fading away.

"Keep singing," Jakob urged Moira.

She needed no urging, starting immediately on "You Are My Sunshine," going from there to three old British songs: "Western Wind," "Hares on the Mountain," and "The Great Selchie of Sule Skerry." She thought she'd have to start on nursery rhymes next, then go back to the beginning if she could only remember what the beginning had consisted of. But she worried repeats might annoy Aenmarr instead of enchanting him. For once she didn't need to tell herself to shut up.

By the time she had come to the last verse of the selchie song—luckily Scottish ballads have more verses than sense—the troll boy, Buri, was back with the guitar and handed it to his father.

That was when Moira's heart sank. Aenmarr couldn't come close enough to the wall of flames to lift the guitar over. And Jakob didn't dare go out of the circle to get it.

Stalemate, she thought. *And just when things seemed to be going* so *well.*

She started to cry, which made singing difficult. And to make matters worse, the bottom part of the circle behind them burned through and everything above it crashed to the ground.

19

Jakob

Jakob ducked as sparks from the collapsing circle showered him. Grabbing Moira, he dragged her toward the center of the ring. She was still singing. Something about a Susie Clellan being burned in Dundee.

Very topical. He hoped Susie made it. Even more, he hoped they did.

"Aenmarr," he called out to the towering troll, "throw the guitar . . . er . . . fiddle."

Aenmarr raised a dark green eyebrow dubiously.

"Don't be an idiot," Moira whispered. "He couldn't reach us with his other projectiles. How's he going to get the guitar in here without breaking it to pieces?"

Jakob looked behind him, thinking the collapse had lowered the wall, but it also made the flames gout higher when fresh oxygen had hit them.

"I can catch it."

"And if you don't? Then where will we be?"

Jakob set his lips in a tight line. "I can catch it."

Moira relented. "All right. I hope you do." Then she returned to the Susie song.

"Okay, Aenmarr, when I count to three. . . ." Jakob squinted through the smoke and flames.

Who are you trying to fool? he thought. *There isn't a fly ball in the world that hasn't hit you on the head.*

"One . . ."

You're going to drop the guitar. Break our only bargaining chip.

"Two . . ."

Stop showing off for the girl and think!

"Wait!" Jakob shouted. "Don't throw it. I . . ." He looked over at Moira and shrugged. "I might drop it."

Moira gave him a wan smile and sang the last line of the Susie song: "And bonnie Susie Clellan was burned in Dundee."

Crud, Jakob thought abruptly. Then he yelled to Aenmarr, "We'll just . . . we'll just have to trust one another. We make a Compact tonight and we will start the lessons tomorrow night when you release the princesses."

Aenmarr's big belly shook with laughter. "Trust? How can I be trusting you? You be allied with the Fossegrim."

"The fox?" Jakob kicked away some smoldering branches. "What's he to us?"

"That I do not be knowing, Little Doom. But you be a fool to be trusting him." The big green eyebrows went up and down as he spoke.

Frowning, Jakob asked, "Why's that?"

Suddenly, an arrow sprouted from Aenmarr's right

shoulder. The troll peered almost matter-of-factly at the feathered shaft as if it were no more nuisance than an insect bite, and snapped it off in his hand.

"Hah!" Aenmarr rumbled. "This be your idea of trust?" Another arrow struck his chest, and he ripped it out with a growl. "I soon be eating your liver, human, eating it while you be still alive!"

Just then Jakob heard Foss in his mind, shouting angrily, "The eyes, you fool! Aim for the eyes!"

To his right, through the flickering fire, Jakob saw Erik stepping from the forest into the clearing. He carried a bow nearly as tall as himself.

"I'm trying," Erik cried out, notching another arrow. "I wasn't a Boy Scout for long." He let fly, and Jakob whipped around to see Aenmarr swat the arrow angrily from the air. "We didn't do much archery."

Not any, Jakob thought, furious with his brother for being so stupid. *And you were actually a* Cub *Scout, and for only a single season before quitting. Dad never forgave you for that. He had to remain scoutmaster the whole year.*

Aenmarr tossed Jakob's guitar to his son and charged. Erik fumbled to notch another arrow into the bow, but the arrow seemed to leap from his trembling hand. And after three big steps, Aenmarr was almost upon him.

Erik dropped his bow and ran.

"Oh, Erik," Jakob cried, looking around frantically for some way to help, but he and Moira were surrounded by flames. He watched helplessly as Erik disappeared into the woods just ahead of Aenmarr. The rampaging troll began ripping trees up by their trunks as he chased in after the boy.

Soon, they were both swallowed by the trees and the darkness, but Jakob could still hear Aenmarr's thunderous footfalls. *If those footsteps stop,* he thought, *I'll know Erik's dead.*

Moira grabbed Jakob by the shoulders. "We have to get out of here. When Aenmarr comes back, I don't think music is going to soothe the savage beast anymore. He's going to pick up one of those tree trunks and sweep our fire away."

She was right, Jakob realized. Again. He tore his eyes away from the dark tree line. "But how do we get out?"

Moira pointed at the section of the bonfire that had collapsed behind them. "Through there."

The flames were still high, but the wall *was* significantly lower. Just not low enough. "There's no way we can jump over that."

"Not right now," Moira said. "But maybe if . . ." Taking off her pot helmet, she heaved it as hard as she could right at the weakened section. It hit with a solid thunk and fell into the flames. A single smoldering branch toppled to the ground but the wall of flame didn't budge.

Moira's shoulders slumped.

They stared into the flames, dejected.

"I have an idea," Jakob said suddenly, stooping to pick up a branch that lay near them. He inched forward on his stomach, holding the branch out in front of him. It was hot, but he forced himself to keep going until he thought his eyebrows would burst into flames. Then he poked and prodded the branch at the bonfire. Hot sparks showered him again and stung the backs of his hands.

"Keep going!" Moira called. "I think it's working."

Encouraged, Jakob poked harder. More sparks kicked

up; smoke roiled. His lungs burned from it, and he could no longer see what he was doing.

Moira most have sensed that he was mometarily blinded, because she began shouting directions. "Now to the left. Up a little. One hard one in the middle. That's it! It's going to . . . oh, no!"

Jakob looked up, then pushed his face into the ground as the flaming bonfire collapsed on top of him. Fire burned his neck, his back, his right leg. He tried to scramble backward, but he was trapped under the hot logs. Trapped and burning. He couldn't do anything but scream into the ground.

Then Moira grabbed his ankles and dragged him from the wreckage, swatting at the flames rising from his shirt and pants. "Roll!" she shouted. "Roll!"

Jakob rolled and rolled until Moira said breathlessly, "They're out. The flames are out." He rolled once more for good measure.

"Owowowowowow," he cried. "Hot."

Moira laughed nervously. "You okay?"

"I don't know." He stumbled to his feet. He hurt everywhere, and he smelled of burnt hair, but it seemed he could move. "Let's get out of here."

There was a gap in the flaming wall, like a missing tooth. Moira eyed it critically. "I think we can make it," she said. "If you can jump."

Jakob flexed his right leg. He nodded, but added, "But maybe not for long."

"We only need one good jump," she told him. "Do you need a hand?"

"No," he said, "just adrenaline!" He began running

toward the breach in the flames. It seemed to grow smaller instead of bigger as he approached, but he didn't slow down.

Neither did Moira.

And then they leaped through the flames and landed on the other side in matching, clumsy shoulder rolls. They kept rolling and rolling to make sure they weren't on fire. At last they came up hard against a giant oak tree where they lay, limbs splayed out, laughing with relief.

They didn't laugh long. Towering over them was the troll boy, Buri, clutching Jakob's guitar.

Moira scrambled to her feet. Jakob's injured leg collapsed under him, and he fell to one knee. Putting his back to the tree, he clenched his fists.

"Run!" he called to Moira.

Instead, Moira assumed a karate stance, calling, "C'mon, you ugly beast. Let's do this."

The young troll let his head drop to one side, puzzled. He held the guitar toward Jakob. "Fiddle, Little Doom," he said, his voice quavering nervously. "Can you be teaching *me* to play?"

Jakob stood, his leg throbbing. For a moment he didn't quite understand what the troll boy was asking. Then he slowly unclenched his fists and glanced over at Moira who was still crouched awkwardly. She managed to shrug.

"Can you teach him to play?" she asked.

"But what about Eric?" Jakob asked. "We have to find him."

"We can't help. We have to trust he'll get away. That Foss will hide him. This is our part of the plan. Jakob—we have to stick with the plan."

He nodded, knowing she was right. He waved at Buri to

hand him the guitar. As he tuned it, he saw Buri's mother begin walking from the house toward them. Behind her came two other troll women. They were big, ugly, and green.

Jakob suppressed a shudder. "All right, Buri," he said, placing his left hand on the guitar. "This is a G chord." He strummed and Buri shivered.

"Oooh," Buri said. "I like that one."

Jakob smiled. "Your turn."

"What?"

Jakob pressed the guitar into Buri's green hands. "It's your turn. Look, your first finger goes here . . ." Jakob placed Buri's fingers in the right position then eyed him critically. "I don't think you'll need a pick with those fingernails." They were long, hard, dirty, and black. "Go ahead and strum."

"Strum?"

"Yes, strum. Like this." Jakob grabbed the troll's hand and swept it down the strings. Moira cringed at the horrendous noise, but Jakob's face showed nothing. He'd heard worse. In fact Galen had sounded at least that awful when he'd started, though not quite as loud. Luckily Buri hadn't broken any strings. Yet. "Not bad, Buri, not bad. Try again."

Buri was grinning from ear to pointed ear as he strummed again. The noise was still horrible, but, Jakob thought, perhaps marginally better than the first attempt. *The little troll might actually learn something. If he doesn't eat his teacher first.*

"Okay, now let me show you a C."

Moira tapped Jakob surreptitiously on the shoulder and whispered. "Here's trouble."

Jakob glanced up fearfully. All three troll women were now gathered around them. They were close enough to touch Moira or grab Jakob. They stank of perspiration and cooking juices. Jakob's hands shook as he placed Buri's hands boldly on an open C and let the chord ring.

All the trolls closed their eyes and the female trolls smiled rapturously.

"Think of it," Buri's mother breathed. "My son, a musician. I could be passing out with the joy of it."

The other two *ooh*ed and *aah*ed as Buri rattled the strings inexpertly. *But,* Jakob thought, *at least he isn't afraid to try, unlike Galen who'd been embarrassed and angry having to learn from his baby brother.* He bit his lip. He mustn't think about Galen now. Or Erik.

Jakob choked back a sudden sob. "Buri, would you . . ." he said as evenly as he could, "would you like to learn a whole song?"

"Oh, yes!" the little troll cried, shoving the guitar back into Jakob's hands. "Yes!"

"Mama, I want to learn, too!" There was a second troll boy now, standing beside the troll wives.

"Be quiet, Arri," said the tallest of the wives.

"No, no," Jakob said quickly, "that can be arranged." He strummed a D. "This is the first song I ever learned on guitar. It's called, 'Hang Down Your Head, Tom Dooley.' If I could learn it, certainly a troll can."

He sang the simple song, and when Moira joined in on harmony at the chorus, Buri's mother sat down heavily.

"My goodness," she said. "It be too beautiful."

The other trolls grunted and snorted in time. And when the song ended, and Jakob told Buri, "Okay, your turn," his mother did, indeed, fall back on the grass in a dead faint.

· 20 ·

Moira

They survived a ragged chorus of "Tom Dooley," with Jakob's hands on Buri's making the guitar strum the open chord. Moira couldn't bring herself to call it music. The noise of it was appalling, but the trolls certainly seemed to love it. They waved their hands and grinned.

Trigvi awoke from her faint at the end of the first chorus, then promptly passed out again. She lay on the grass with such a beatific smile, Moira figured it was a troll's version of Heaven.

By the second chorus, Trigvi was back on her feet and singing along huskily. *If,* Moira thought, *that bizarre organization of notes can be considered singing. Though, it's wonderful to have such an extreme response to music.*

All of the troll women clapped against the beat and lifted their knees one at a time, then twirled around. It was as if mountains danced. Perspiration like huge cultured pearls popped out on their foreheads. It was disgusting, but at least they seemed happy. And not preparing a soup of human meat. All of which was not to be despised.

"Now," Jakob said to the troll boys, "I will teach you a new note."

"But I be loving this one," Buri said, strumming the C chord again. "Hang down, Tom! Hang down!" His voice was like a buzz saw.

Arri sang with him. *Or rather,* Moira thought, *Arri is singing after him, about a beat too late. And on a different note. Even*—she made a face—*a different scale.*

"Ah," Jakob said, "That *is* a good note, Buri. A very good one. You're right to like it so much. It's a favorite of mine, too. All musicians love C. Isn't that right, Moira?"

Moira nodded.

Buri grinned. His teeth—and there seemed far too many of them—were very sharp.

Arri grinned, too. "I be liking C, I do, I do."

"Be quiet, Arri," warned Selvi.

Jakob nodded at her with a kind of conspiratorial look. "But as your mothers know, there are more, even better notes still to come."

Selvi nodded. "Better. Better," she murmured in a kind of chant. "Better, better."

"Oh, oh, oh," Botvi cried, her meaty hands on her breast. "If only Oddi is being here. He be loving notes. I be missing my little Oddi."

"Better notes," Trigvi interrupted. "We be wanting better notes." Her voice was one big demand.

Moira didn't know what Jakob was planning—or even if

he was planning anything—but she thought he needed some help. "If I could learn those notes," she said, "why a troll could learn them, too." She said it softly and with a smile.

Jakob grinned at her, then at Buri and Arri.

The troll wives all chorused, "A troll can. Of course, of course."

"Let me play you some tunes in that new note," Jakob suggested. He did a quick run on the guitar and Moira approved. It was clean and crisp and perfectly in tune. Then he did a jazz syncopation in E, his fingers flying over the strings. One by one, the trolls wives' eyes glazed over, and they toppled like redwoods. The troll boys teetered, but didn't fall.

What now? Moira mouthed at Jakob.

He held one finger up—a wait-and-see gesture.

First Trigvi, then Botvi, and finally Selvi woke up.

"That be wonderful, Little Doom," Selvi said.

"Let's go into the house where we can sit down," Jakob told them. "And I will show Buri and Arri how to play the next special note. Because it's not a standing-up note, but a sitting-down note." Turning, he winked slyly at Moira.

"Ah!" Now she got it: He was planning to herd them all into one house and entrance them with the music, giving her time to sneak into the other houses and wake the girls and . . .

Botvi picked up Jakob like a baby, and carried him in her arms toward the houses. Meanwhile, Trigvi grabbed Moira by her right arm like a rag doll, dangling her awkwardly, and banging her against her right leg, a leg as big around as a tree trunk. The two boy trolls took turns carrying the guitar, as if it were a great trophy. Selvi being the oldest and first wife led the way to her own house. Clearly if any music was going to be made, it would be there.

This close to Trigvi, Moira was almost sick from the stink of troll. The odor was a heavy musk. *Like an ox,* Moira thought. She'd smelled one of those in the London zoo the summer her orchestra toured through Europe. Like wild oxen, the wives smelled meaty, sweaty, dangerous, unpredictable. *And they're green, which is really weird.* She tried to hold her breath. Finally, they entered the house, where Trigvi dropped Moira onto the floor. Luckily, she landed on her feet.

She recognized the room, of course, with its wall full of hideous skulls, horns and antlers sticking out of them from improbable places. The dark cauldron, big as a hot tub, swung on its iron arm. She didn't dare look at the wooden box where she knew Susie, Caitlinn, Maddie, and Dylinn lay in their enchanted sleep.

Botvi set Jakob on the sofa, and the troll boys lowered the guitar into his lap with great ceremony.

"The next note," they begged together.

"Please," added Buri, surely not a word often used by trolls.

"Wait—we must be having food and drink," Selvi said. "For this special time."

Trigvi and Botvi agreed, and they hustled into the larder where they banged about. Moira was really afraid of what they'd bring out to eat.

"Arri," Selvi called, "go be cutting down your stepbrother. He can be singing 'Tom Drool' with us. And be hearing Little Doom's second note. He will be liking that."

"I will, Mama!" Arri cried, running swiftly out of the room and into the hallway that led to the bedroom.

Jakob and Moira looked at one another. *Stepbrother? There were* more *trolls?*

Moira started to panic. Would this throw a monkey wrench into their plan? *As if we have a plan,* she thought. What if the stepbrother was a bigger troll? Or has a head full of horns like the skulls on the wall? And why had he been tied up? Was he dangerous, even to trolls? Moira's head buzzed with questions, though she didn't actually want to know the answers to any of them. Except a last question: *Will the music work on him the way it does on the wives?* Suddenly she was more afraid than she'd been before.

Just then she heard a *thud* and a *thump* and a loud, "Arri, you little bugger, that hurt!" from the bedroom. And the sound of Arri giggling.

Well, at least the stepbrother could talk. *Is that good news,* she wondered, *or bad?* She glanced over at Jakob and was astonished to see that his head had rocked back and his mouth dropped open. His eyes had gotten as big as marbles and he was staring past her.

"Are you all right?" she asked. But then she heard a noise from the hallway and turned to see what he was staring at.

A tall, slender boy with high cheekbones and a dimple in his chin was standing there, raking his hands through his dark fall of hair. He was handsome and, as far as she could tell, entirely human. Arri was by his side looking down at him adoringly, the way a child looks at its puppy or cat.

"Galen . . ." Jakob whispered, choking back a sob.

"Why, hello, little brother," Galen said matter-of-factly.

"I thought you were dinner."

Galen laughed. "Oh, I'm much too pretty for dinner," he said. "Isn't that right, Mama Selvi?" He dimpled at her.

"And he sings," Selvi said. She looked ready to faint again.

"Oh, for pity's sake." Moira was suddenly disgusted with the whole Griffson family. Her right arm hurt, she needed a shower, her friends were in boxes, time was growing short, and the boys were being . . . well, boys!

Only then did Galen notice her. He smiled with enormous charm.

Moira glared back at him. She was not impressed.

· 21 ·

Jakob

"Galen!" Jakob said again. "How did you . . . ?"

"Like Mama Selvi says," Galen said. "I sing."

"But . . ."

"Upside down in the larder, to keep my spirits up."

"It probably improved the timbre," Jakob said.

"Maybe we should talk about this later." Galen's usually smooth voice had a ragged edge, as if it had torn on a nail.

It was only then that Jakob noticed the haggard look in Galen's eyes and realized how hard his brother must be working to keep up his charming nonchalance.

"Note, note, note," Buri and Arri chanted.

Jakob glanced up at them. "Your mothers said food first. Then note." He plinked a few chords on the guitar—just a teaser. "Think you could help them out? Might speed things up."

"Oh, what an idea!" Buri cried.

"We be going at once!" Arri added, and they scampered into the larder.

If, Jakob thought, *that lead-footed run could be called a scamper.* As soon as they were out of the room, he leapt to his feet, guitar in hand. "Quickly, now!" he whispered. "The girls!"

"What?" Galen said, staring blankly at Moira as she pushed past him and leapt into a large wooden box standing open near the central table.

"Pretty boy," she called to him. "Get over here!"

Standing, Jakob tested his leg. It seemed to be holding up as long as he didn't put too much weight on it. He limped over to the larder door, hoping to block the troll's view of the living room. But it became quickly obvious that blocking wasn't going to work. The trolls were head and shoulders taller than he was. *Several heads and shoulders.* He was going to have to use misdirection. Looking inside the larder, he saw that Trigvi and Botvi were pulling haunches of meat off huge hooks and presenting them to Selvi, who poked and prodded and sniffed at each before shaking her head no. The troll boys were playing with knives. "Can I play a little something while you prepare supper, ladies?"

"Oh, yes!" came the immediate answer. "Play!"

Jakob started fingerpicking a random chord progression, occasionally glancing into the living room where Moira had climbed into the box. After only two measures on his guitar, Moira's head popped back up. Then her shoulders and arms appeared as she grunted and heaved an unconscious girl over the edge of the box and into Galen's unsuspecting arms.

"What?" he said, bending under the sudden burden.

"You're not getting any smarter, are you, pretty boy?" she said acidly.

Galen eased the sleeping princess to the floor. "No need to . . . oof." Another girl dropped into his arms.

Jakob hissed at them to be quieter, then glanced back into the larder. The troll women were now flailing away at unidentifiable haunches of meat with cleavers and knives, while Buri and Arri scampered around their legs in a rough game of tag. Evidently food trumped music, for none of them were fainting.

"Hurry, hurry, hurry," Jakob sang, loud enough for Moira to hear. "For dinner might be soon."

"Hurry! Hurry! Hurry!" the troll boys sang back, thinking the message was for them. They were a half step apart and both flat.

Botvi, Selvi, and Trigvi kept on chopping.

Shooting Jakob an exasperated look, Moira picked up a third girl from the box before disappearing again. The fourth girl followed soon thereafter, and then Moira heaved herself out as well. Jakob looked to his right at the girls stacked like so much cordwood on the floor, then looked to his left at the big front door.

The *closed* front door.

"What now?" Jakob sang. "Hurry."

"Hurry, Buri," Arri sang back.

Buri giggled.

Now the troll boys' game of tag began to take on a frantic pace, and Selvi looked down at them, frowning.

Meanwhile in the living room, Moira followed Jakob's

gaze to the closed door and frowned. Poking Galen, she said, "Make yourself useful, tall guy. Open that door."

Galen gave her the smile that Jakob had once heard Erik call, "teeny-bopper's bane."

"My pleasure, young lady," he said and took off across the room. Moira rolled her eyes. Jakob swung his head around in time to see his brother take a running leap at the door.

And come up a foot short of the latch.

"I can do it," Galen said immediately and backed up.

"Well, do it quickly," Moira replied.

Jakob began singing louder to cover their noise. The louder he sang, the faster Arri and Buri ran around the table. Now Selvi had her hands on her hips. But Trigvi and Botvi had stopped chopping food and were listening to the singing, closing their eyes, and swaying, as if ready to faint.

Galen took another run at the front door, and got closer this time, but it was obvious to Jakob that his brother wasn't going to be able to reach the latch. Then Galen tried one last time, coming down noisy and hard after barely brushing the latch with his fingertips.

"What be that?" Selvi called looking over at Jakob.

For a moment Jakob couldn't think of an answer.

"What be that?" Selvi asked again, wiping her hands on her apron and starting toward him.

"Nothing, Mama Selvi," Galen called from the living room floor. "Just me being clumsy."

Jakob swore that the big troll wife actually tittered. She fluttered her eyelids, practically making a gale. "Oh, Galen," she called back, "you be graceful as a deer, not clumsy." She turned back to the chopping block.

Galen pushed himself painfully to his feet. "Sorry," he mouthed.

Moira looked to Jakob. He thought frantically. *We need someone to open the door.* He looked around the room. *But only the trolls are big enough.* For a moment he stopped singing and Botvi and Trigvi opened their eyes. He began to tremble. *Quick, Quick,* he told himself, *Think, Jakob. Think of a reason why would we need to go outside.* Frantically he looked around. *Ah—I don't see a bathroom.*

"Um . . . Mama Selvi?" Jakob called into the larder. "I need to go to the bathroom."

"The what room?" she replied.

Do they not go? he thought. Then, *No, they just don't know what a bathroom is.* "I need to . . . um . . ." He made a gesture with his thumb and first finger.

"Ah, Arri! Be bringing our musician the basin."

"Yes, Mother," came the reply and Arri rushed out of the larder, almost knocking Jakob over in the process. Sparing one confused glance at the princesses stacked up on the floor, the young troll charged into the bedroom, returning moments later with a huge, foul-smelling basin. He plopped it down in front of Jakob and waited expectantly.

"I . . . um . . ." Jakob stuttered.

"He can't go over the top of that, Arri," Galen said. "See how small he is?"

Thank you, big brother. "Yeah, I'm too small. I'm the little brother. I'll have to go outside."

Arri shrugged. Then glancing once more at the enchanted Dairy Princesses, he walked to the front door and pushed it open.

Everyone just stared at each other for a moment.

Jakob said, "Okay . . . I guess I'll . . ."

"Arri," Moira interrupted. "Shouldn't you go back and help your mother and aunts?"

The troll boy blinked. "Oh, yes! We be having so much fun cooking. You will love what we be making. A very special meal, indeed!"

"Yeah, Arri," Jakob said. "That sounds great. Now, hurry, so we can eat and then I can teach you those new notes!"

Arri nodded, beamed, and dashed back into the larder, singing, "New note, new note."

"Everyone grab a girl," said Moira. "Pretty boy, you get two." She looked grimly at Jakob. "Now, let's get out of here."

Jakob should have been elated: they were steps away from freedom. But instead he was thinking about Erik running into the woods with Aenmarr right behind him. *And the seven other Dairy Princesses? What could be done about them?*

Then he shoved those thoughts to the back of his mind, and hooked one of the Dairy Princesses under her arms. His guitar still in one hand, he dragged her backward toward the door, his leg screaming in pain. He prayed fervently that it would hold his weight, that Erik was still alive, that none of the troll wives would look out the larder door and see them all leaving. They didn't seem quite as stupid as the young trolls.

He needn't have worried about the last bit; a quick glance into the larder showed the troll women completely engrossed in their task of molding raw meat into the shape of a large fox.

And besides, he never reached the door.

Something heavy hit him in the back and tumbled him over. He dropped the girl with a *thud,* and rolled, trying to protect his guitar from smashing to bits. His neck and back flared in agony as he pushed himself upright to see what had knocked him over.

It was Erik. He was obviously hurt, with blood and dirt caking his face. The bruise under his eye was now deep purple with streaks of yellow. But he was alive!

"Erik!" Jakob cried. "How did you get away?"

Erik cranked open his eyes and looked at Jakob blearily. "I didn't," he croaked, before slumping to the floor.

Jakob looked up. And up. And up. Aenmarr filled the doorway, a short tree trunk in one hand, the stub of an arrow still sticking out of his right shoulder.

"Why be all my wives in the larder," Aenmarr rumbled, "when all the meat be in the main hall?" Then roaring with laughter, he stepped inside the house, slamming the great door shut behind him.

5 · Doom, Gloom, and After

∽

The goose flies past the setting sun,
Plums roasting in her breast,
Sleeping Beauty lays her head down,
A hundred years to rest.
And fee-fi-fo the giant fums,
And to my dark Prince Charming comes
A-ride, ride, riding.
Into my night of darkness
My own Prince Charming comes.

The witch is popped into the oven,
Rising into cake,
The swan queen glides her downy form,
To the enchanted lake.
And rum-pum-pum the drummer drums,
As into darkness my prince comes
A-ride, ride, riding.
Into my night of darkness
My own Prince Charming comes.

It's half past twelve and once again
The shoe of glass is gone,
And magic is as magic was,
And vanished with the dawn.
For Pooh has hummed his final hum,
The giant finished off his fums,
They've drawn their final breath,
For into darkness my prince comes
A-ride, ride, riding.
For into darkness my prince comes,
On his bony horse called Death.

—Words and music by
Jakob and Erik Griffson,
featuring Moira Darr on lead vocals,
from *Troll Bridge*

Radio WMSP: 10:00 A.M.

"So, Jim, here it is Friday morning, or as our ancestors used to say, 'Frigga's Day.'"

"Your ancestors, Katie. My ancestors are English. We say 'TGIF.'"

"[Laughs.] But to be real serious now, Jim, do you have any news for us on the Vanderby story about the missing Dairy Princesses. And The Griffson Brothers?"

"Why yes, Katie, there's another strange occurrence to report. A huge fire—or at least a lot of smoke—spiraled up above the forest on the other side of the little stone bridge where the teenagers were known to have disappeared. The local fire department—all volunteers, dontcha know—tramped through those woods looking for the source of the fire, hoping it might be from a campfire started by the kids. But they found nothing. Not a fire, not an ember, nothing."

"Curiouser and curiouser, Jim, as Harry Potter would say."

"I think that's *Alice in Wonderland, Katie.*"

"*You may be right, Jim. I don't read fantasy books. Just give me the facts, ma'am. That's* Dragnet, *by the way. What did the fire chief have to say?*"

"*He said . . .*"

<click>

"*It's a riddle wrapped in a mystery inside an enigma, Jim.*"

<click>

"*That sounds like a quote, too.*"

"*It's Churchill, Katie. The chief is a history professor in Duluth. But I have more.*"

"*More from the chief?*"

"*No, Katie, from the oldest resident of Vanderby, the official gold cane holder.*"

"*And who is that, Jim?*"

"*His name is Olaf Gunnerson and he spoke to me this morning, right before going to his hundred-and-fifth birthday party in the nursing home.*"

<click>

"*I am Olaf Gunnerson and I am a hundred and five today. And I want to say that those missing kids are probably in Trollholm. With the trolls. My mother used to say that whenever anyone disappeared around here. You know, run off or something.*"

<click>

"*So between the mayor's terrorists and Mr. Gunnerson's trolls we have . . .*"

"*No real news, Katie.*"

"*Thanks, Jim, and now we'll get Bob to give us the sports.*"

"*Hi, Katie, Bob here, we could sure use some tree-tall trolls to help the Timberwolves, who just dropped their fifth straight game in a row.*"

· 22 ·

Jacob

Strung up once more, Jakob listened to Moira squabbling with his brothers as they all swung head-down in the larder.

"Ow."

"Quit banging into me."

"I'm not doing it on purpose."

"My head hurts."

"Shut up!"

"Why? Are they going to eat us for being too loud?"

"They're going to eat us anyway."

Jakob couldn't even tell who was talking anymore. Their voices all sounded the same, a dull background buzz to accompany the final few hours of his short life.

What a waste, he thought. *Going through all that just to end back here, hung from hooks like four slabs of ham.*

They'd tried to fight Aenmarr. Jakob had thought Moira particularly brave, flailing and biting and scratching at the big troll's leathery green skin. But he'd just laughed and scooped them up like recalcitrant children. Within seconds they'd been trussed securely and hung upside down over the blood-stained table that had so recently held a meat statue of a giant fox.

The fox!

Jakob found his voice again. "Hey." The others went on arguing. "Hey!"

Moira was the first to stop. "What is it, Jakob?"

Jakob wriggled around until he could see her. Her face was an alarming red. "We have to contact the fox."

"Foss? Think he can get us out of here?" Moira's shoulders strained as she tried to free her hands. Jakob knew the rope wouldn't budge. He'd tried already. Aenmarr tied a mean knot.

"I don't know what Foss can do," he answered. "Or even what he would do. But he's our only hope now."

Moira nodded, an odd gesture upside down. Then she winced. "My head hurts."

"Never mind that," Erik said with a groan. "Let's all concentrate. Send the little red guy a message."

"What do you mean?" Galen asked.

"Foss," Erik said. "Call him."

"Sorry, left my cell phone in the car."

Suddenly Jakob realized that Galen really didn't know what they meant. He'd never met Foss. He might not even be musician enough to hear the fox's words in his mind. They'd have to work without him.

"All right." Jakob watched as Moira and Eric squeezed their eyes shut, then did the same. He concentrated hard, picturing his thoughts leaping out of his body and shooting through the air to the fox's cave, or wherever he was at the moment. Pictured the fox turning and sniffing the air, pricking up his ears.

"What *are* you guys doing?" Galen asked. "Shouldn't we be trying to get loose? I'll try Mama Trigvi . . ."

But they ignored him.

Foss, Jakob thought at him. *Oh great, Fossegrim. We who have assisted you in the return of your fiddle, we who have been soldiers in your fight against Aenmarr, we need your help now. Without assistance, all is lost. I know you are a clever creature. Think of something, please. Get us out of here!*

Jakob opened his eyes. Saw the others slowly opening theirs. Sending one last *Please!* out into the ether, he asked, "Anyone get through?"

"Blank as a troll's brain," Erik said, shrugging, which was hard to do with the ropes pulled so tight.

"I don't know," Moira said. "It almost felt as if he were listening, but I can't be sure." She shook her head. It didn't look quite as odd upside down as nodding had. "I didn't hear anything back from him, though."

They all glanced at Galen. "I don't have a clue to what you're talking about. I was just praying."

"What now?" Erik asked.

Jakob didn't answer, because just then the larder door crashed open and Aenmarr strode in.

"I be deciding to kill you first, Little Doom," he said. "What you be saying to that?"

Jakob's heart leapt into his throat, and he was suddenly sweating. Actually, he couldn't think of anything to say.

Striding to the wall, Aenmarr very deliberately plucked a giant cleaver from the pegs. He tested its edge with his thumb. "Do you be having any last requests?"

"Well, actually I . . ." Jakob began.

Aenmarr interrupted him, roaring, "Well, too bad!" while whipping the cleaver back for an overhand stroke that Jakob knew would easily split him in two.

Moira screamed. Galen, too.

Jakob squeezed his eyes shut, not daring to watch the final blow come down. He thought he heard Erik breathe, "I'm sorry," but his heart was pounding too loud for him to hear clearly. Gritting his teeth, he waited for the sharp pain of the cleaver's edge.

It never came.

Jakob opened one eye to see Selvi holding Aenmarr's wrist.

"What," Aenmarr said to her very slowly. "Be. You. Doing?"

"I . . . uh . . ." she stammered. Finally she blurted out: "They be musicians!" She took a deep breath, never letting go of her husband's wrist. "Doom be teaching my son the guitar." She smiled up at her husband, and Aenmarr's ugly green face softened. "*Our* son."

"Our son? A musician?" he breathed, pointing at Jakob. "He be saying that?"

Selvi nodded. "He be . . ."

Jakob assumed she would have kept speaking, but all the air was suddenly forced out of her lungs by Aenmarr's boulder-sized fist hitting her in the midsection. She crumpled to the ground.

"Foolish old woman," he said. "You be daring to oppose my will? In my own house?" He winked at Jakob. "Women, eh?" Then he hefted his cleaver again. "Now, where be we?"

Jakob didn't even have time to squeeze his eyes shut before Trigvi leapt into the room, throwing herself in front of him.

"No, Aenmarr! We be having a chance for our sons to—" That was as far as she got before she, too, took a shot from Aenmarr and fell over.

The troll boys scampered in next crying, "Daddy, Daddy, no!"

Aenmarr slapped them into silence till they cowered next to their mothers.

Jakob heard low sobs coming from behind him. Moira was crying.

"You . . . monster," she gasped.

Aenmarr turned, glared at her. Then he smiled an ear-to-pointed-ear grin that showed off his long, sharp teeth. "Exactly, little princess."

Trigvi and Selvi stirred on the floor, and Moira called out to them. "How can you let him treat you that way? How can you let him treat your children that way?"

Neither of the wives on the floor answered, but Botvi suddenly filled the doorway.

"Because he be protecting us," she said quietly.

Moira snorted. "Protecting you from what?"

"From him." Botvi pointed at Jakob. "Aenmarr be telling me now. Killer of my son!" A single swamp-green tear rolled down her cheek. "Killer of my Oddi."

Jakob nodded, tears of his own suddenly filling his eyes as he remembered Oddi's death. "I didn't mean to."

Trigvi and Selvi got shakily to their feet. They turned hurt eyes at him. Hurt and angry.

"How did you be not meaning to?" Botvi accused.

"I . . . I . . ." Jakob said.

"Enough!" bellowed Aenmarr, raising the cleaver again.

Jakob yelled back, "I tricked Oddi, yes. So it was my fault he died." Jakob wished he could point an accusatory finger at Aenmarr, but his hands were tied behind his back. "But it was your husband who killed him."

"That be nonsense," said Aenmarr. "I be killing no one since that young prince for the stew the night before last, Botvi."

"Not for lack of trying," Erik muttered.

Botvi stared straight ahead. "The last night we be seeing Oddi."

"Did you notice," Jakob said, "that the prince you killed looked a lot like me, Aenmarr?"

"You all look alike: sweet meat wrapped in pale flesh," Aenmarr said.

"Oddi and I traded places. He cast a spell to disguise himself and then leapt up on the hook. That wasn't me you cut into pieces for stew." Jakob wriggled, trying to fix Aenmarr with a hard stare. He kept spinning away and had to call over his shoulder, "It was your own son you killed. Chopped, stewed, and ate."

"No . . ." Aenmarr looked at Jakob then back at Botvi. "No. You be telling lies."

Botvi peered at Jakob, her green eyes nearly popping out. "He do be looking like that dinner, husband." She turned to

Selvi and Trigvi who were pushing themselves to their feet. "I be thinking Little Doom tells the truth."

"It be nothing," Aenmarr said and almost casually slapped Botvi. She flew back into the wall, shaking the cottage timbers as she hit. "All princes be looking the same." He pointed the cleaver at Jakob. "My son be killed by this pitiful creature. And now, if you hags be done screeching, he be dying by my hand."

Selvi and Trigvi looked to Botvi who was picking herself up off the floor. She shook herself once all over, and then said, "Get him, girls."

Aenmarr's eyes widened in astonishment.

Selvi hit him high, and Trigvi low, riding him to the floor. Screaming, Botvi leapt on his arm, wrestling the cleaver from his grasp. Aenmarr roared and threw the three troll women off, but they were back in seconds, scratching and biting and clawing and digging at his eyes.

Aenmarr came to his feet, troll wives hanging from his arms and legs. He pummeled them, swatted at them, fists like sacks of coal. Still, Jakob could see they were hurting him. Green blood oozed from dozens of claw and teeth marks, and he was grimacing with each new wound.

"Enough, women!" he roared, but to no avail. Their fury had no end. They kept attacking, coming at him nonstop, even though their eyes began to swell shut, their faces bleed. Selvi's arm was hanging crooked and useless at her side, obviously broken.

Aenmarr threw them off a tenth time. A twentieth. Jakob lost count. But finally the old troll was done fighting. Turning his back on the larder, he stomped into the main room, his three wives screaming behind him. From where he was hanging in the larder, Jakob could just see the front door. He watched as Aenmarr pushed it open, trying to get out of the house, trying to escape his wives' wrath. But strangely, he didn't step outside.

He stopped cold in the doorway, and said, simply, "Oh, no."

Then Selvi, Trigvi, and Botvi all pushed him hard at the very same time, Botvi swinging a frying pan at his head with her other hand, and he tumbled out of the house. The troll women quickly moved away from the doorway, and Jakob could suddenly see outside, where the morning sun, a perfect blood-red half circle, was just peeking over the horizon.

Leaping up, his face panic-stricken, Aenmarr tried to run back inside. But as he lifted his right leg, a single ray of sunlight touched his knee.

Jakob heard a terrible grinding sound, like a hasp on marble. As he watched, Aenmarr's leg turned hard and gray and motionless.

Stone, Jakob thought. *He's turning to stone. The old tales are true!*

Staring at his stone leg, Aenmarr tried to take a hop-step with the other. But sunlight now shone on that one, too, and in less than an eyeblink, it was stone, as well. Aenmarr could only watch in horror as light began creeping up his body, turning his torso slowly to granite as the sun crested the horizon. Then he looked into the house to where Jakob was hanging upside down, and laughed.

"Well, you be my doom after all," the troll called. "You be

succeeding where thousands tried and failed. You be defeating Aenmarr of Austraegir, slayer of heroes, killer of kings." His voice was getting softer as the sun reached his arms and shoulders, as it kept climbing, transforming everything it touched to cold, gray, stone. "But beware the Fossegrim, Little Doom. For I would only eat your flesh." Aenmarr coughed feebly as daylight hit his neck and his throat began to petrify. "That one be taking your very soul." Then bright sunlight hit the troll full in the face and the last of his green skin turned gray.

Selvi shut the door, and she and her two sisters collapsed against it, all of them bleeding onto the rough floorboards.

23

Moira

"Mama, Mama!" cried the troll boys, picking themselves off the larder floor and racing over to their mothers who lay against the front door. They held their mothers' hands, weeping piteously.

"Arri, Buri . . ." Jakob called. "Come here. Cut us down."

Erik joined him, shouting. "Here, boys, come here."

Galen added, "Come on, you silly buggers. . . ."

The troll boys were too overcome with their own weeping to listen.

Moira forced herself to wriggle until she spun about, bumping into first Galen, then Erik.

"Ow."

"Quit banging into me."

"This time I'm doing it on purpose."

"My head hurts."

"Shut up and listen."

"Why? It's one troll down and five to go, but only if they cut us down first."

"Sing," Moira said to them.

"What?" they asked together.

Jakob had spun around, too, and now all four of them were facing inward, staring at one another.

Like four hams in a butcher shop, Moira thought, almost giggling. *And that's what we really need now—to be hams and overact.* She shook her head. *Okay, so now I'm officially hysterical.*

"She's right, you know. If we sing to them, they'll do anything for us."

"Sing?" Erik said. "What should we sing?"

Jakob shrugged. "Hey—we're the Griffson Brothers. We can control fifty thousand people at a stadium concert with our music. What's two troll boys?"

Erik growled, "The crowd doesn't want to serve us for supper. That's what." His purpled eye glared at Jakob.

But Galen said smoothly, "Let's start with 'Luv U,' and then segue right into 'E-mail' and then 'After Me, Deluge De-love.'" He nodded at Jakob. "Give us the beat."

"One, two, one, two, three . . ." Jakob began. And then, a bit raggedly—because they had no instruments and were hanging upside down and their throats were raw from shouting—the three boys began to sing.

Suddenly, Moira realized that she'd heard those songs before. On the radio, as she fiddled with the dial, looking for a classical station when she was on the road. And when the Dairy Princesses were practicing their walks, books on their heads. And in the van going from photo op to photo op, because Caitlinn always had that music blaring from her iPod.

The Griffson Brothers. She would have hit her head with her hand if she'd been able to move her arms at all. *I suppose I should have recognized the name.* She shook her head. *But it's pop music!* And she shuddered.

First Arri, then Buri looked over at them, Buri scrubbing at his runny nose with the back of his hand. Then, almost as if mesmerized, the troll boys got up, walked over, and stood in the larder listening.

When the third song ended, Buri said, "That be a lot of notes."

"And I can teach all of them to you," Jakob said, wriggling around until he was facing them. "And more."

"More?" Buri and Arri stood beneath the hanging humans, their mouths gaping open. "There be more?"

"Only," Moira added, doing her own wriggling, "you have to get us all down, first."

"All right," Arri said, still glazed from the music.

Buri picked up the cleaver and swung it so wildly near Galen's feet, it nearly took off his shoe.

"Careful," Moira cried. Then she added, "Maybe a knife would be safer."

"Yeah," Galen said, "don't want to be like your father."

Buri rubbed his head, which might have been bruised from Aenmarr's blows, but with the green skin it was hard to tell. "I not be like my father," he said.

"Not at all," Moira told him softly. "Now the knife . . ."

Buri dropped the cleaver with a clatter and picked up a knife, sawing away until Galen dropped onto the table.

"Ow!" Galen complained. "How about a softer landing?"

"I do not be knowing that. Be it a song?" Buri asked.

"Yah," Eric said. "It goes . . ." and he began to sing to the tune of "Three Blind Mice." "Three bound boys, make lots of noise. Cut them down, without a sound. Give them a landing that's soft and is kind. They'll help you all out when you're next in a bind. So get me a knife of my own, and you'll find, we're three unbound boys."

"Be singing more notes," Buri said, sawing through the rope holding Galen's wrists.

Arri got another knife from the pegs and cut down Jakob, who kept singing "You Are My Sunshine" at the top of his lungs.

AT THE SAME TIME, GALEN managed to get both Moira and Erik onto the table without dropping them from the height, then sawed through the ropes binding them. When the four were free, they sat on the table's edge, swinging their feet, and rubbing their wrists and shoulders.

Moira hopped down first. "Arri, Buri, get me some washcloths and soak them in water."

The boys rushed to do her bidding, coming back with dripping cloths, which Moira had to wring out on the floor since she couldn't reach the sink. It was no easy task since the cloths were as large as bath towels.

"I'll take care of your mothers. You take the princes to the other houses and carry all the Dairy Princesses here. Be careful not to hurt them."

"But Moira, they can't go out until dark," Jakob reminded her.

"Then you're on your own, Griffsons."

"We usually are," Galen said. "Come on, guys." They went toward the back door, which Arri and Buri swung open, careful not to let a bit of the sunlight touch their own hands.

Moira headed, instead, toward the front door where the troll wives still lay, stunned and bleeding. She knelt down to tend them.

"Going somewhere?" The familiar voice slid into her head. She looked up. "Foss!"

He'd insinuated himself past the gray stone Aenmarr and through the open door, his ears pricked up, his long tail fluffed out. Sunlight made his coat gleam.

"Where *were* you? Why didn't you help us?" Moira asked.

"I was recovering. You seem to have done just fine without me."

"It was a close thing, Foss," Jakob said. Moira could hear the suspicion in his voice. "We could have used a distraction or three."

Arri hid himself behind Jakob. "Papa be saying not to trust . . ."

"Papa is dead," the fox said bluntly. "He's a big rock in your front yard. You can use him for a climbing stone."

One of the troll wives behind Moira groaned.

Foss trotted over somewhat daintily, stared down at them, and growled.

"Don't you growl at them," Moira said, shaking her finger in his face. "Without them we'd be lunch."

"Take the cleaver and cut off their heads," Foss told her.

"Will not."

Tilting his head to one side, Foss blinked up at her, his

dark eyes giving nothing away. "No matter. Fetch my fiddle."

"Why?"

"Why?" Foss yipped. "It is time to go home, child."

Home! A single tear sprang up in Moira's eye, and she angrily wiped it away. "All right," she told him, "I'd love to get out of here." Turning to Jakob, she said, "I'm going back to the cave for the fiddle."

He nodded. "Good. We'll get the princesses."

Selvi groaned from the front door. "Do not be leaving us with the Fossegrim."

Foss growled at her, the hair on his back bristling, and Moira snapped at him, "Foss! Enough. Just let us go home. Settle your own problems after we leave."

With a low whine, Foss lay down in the corner by the fire and commenced licking his front paw. "Very well, child. Get the fiddle."

"I'm going, I'm going." She thought a minute. There was something in his casual acceptance that felt wrong. She turned to Jakob. "I think you'd better stay here and watch him."

He shrugged, nodded. Looked puzzled, head to one side. But she didn't say any more. She didn't dare. Then she turned back and tried to give a reassuring smile to the troll wives. "Foss can't hurt you." She hoped she was right.

Without waiting for an answer, she went bounding outside just as if she hadn't spent the night leaping through fires and hanging upside down in a troll's larder. She spared a quick glance to the mound of gray stone next to the front door, then ran down the path toward the cave.

First the fiddle. Then—home!

24

Jakob

With Galen and Erik out collecting princesses, and the trolls eyeing Foss warily, the cottage was suddenly quiet. Jakob crawled up into one of the giant chairs, the smallest one. Leaning back against the rough wood, he waited for his head to stop pounding.

It didn't. His head ached, his back burned, his right leg felt like it was going to break in half.

I just want to get home, he thought. *To Mom. To Dad. I'll sleep for a week.* Even after the longest road trip he'd never felt this tired. Of course, even after the longest road trip, he'd never been almost burned alive and nearly eaten by trolls.

"Soon," Foss said in his head. "Soon."

Jakob eyed the fox lying in the corner. Aenmarr had seemed so sure that Foss was not to be trusted. *And he did trick us into coming here to Trollholm.* But he'd saved Jakob's life after that. And Erik's. And he probably would have saved Galen's, too, if he'd known Gale was alive.

And besides, Jakob thought, *why should I trust the word of a troll who'd been trying to kill me for days?*

He bit his lower lip, remembering that the troll wives were afraid of Foss. And Moira had seemed odd about him, too. And . . . there was something else, something that Jakob couldn't quite get.

"Hey, Foss," he said.

"Hmm?" the fox answered, opening one dark eye and looking at Jakob.

"How's that fiddle going to get us home?"

Foss opened his other eye. "I am going to teach you and the girl child how to play it."

Jakob chuckled. "I don't think either of us can learn to play the fiddle in an afternoon."

"It is a magic fiddle." Lifting his head up off his paws, Foss stared at Jakob with his dark eyes. It was like staring into black fathomless pools. "A magic fiddle—and *you* are a musician."

"Yes, but . . ."

"Tell me, child of man, do you not hear music all the time? Music such that you cannot keep your toes from tapping, your lips from whistling, your fingers from tracing the lines of your chosen instrument in the air?"

Jakob had never thought of it that way, but he nodded.

Foss nodded back. "Then you are a musician. And so is the girl." The fox's lips pulled back from his teeth in an animal grin. "And I am the Fossegrim, a teacher of musicians.

I will teach you to play such music as to make the lame to dance and graybeards spring up from the chimney corner."

"Okay," Jakob said, though that was a bizarre thing to want: graybeards and the lame dancing and springing. "But why do we both need to learn? And for what reason?"

"It will take two of you all day to do what the Fossegrim could do in an eyeblink."

"Do what, exactly?" Jakob asked.

"Give me back my true form." Foss sighed. "I have not felt an instrument under my fingers in far too long."

"But why couldn't we do this before? We had the fiddle. All we had to do was fiddle away happily under the waterfall." Sitting up, he glared at Foss. "Only you were so bent on killing the trolls that you risked all our lives while I was negotiating our way out."

Foss laid his head back on his paws as if dismissing Jakob's concerns. He did everything but yawn. "I am sorry for misleading you, child of man. Aenmarr may very well have let you go. But he did more than just take my fiddle; he wrapped me in spells that tied me to this form and to this land. And as long as he lived, he would never have released me. Both the fiddle *and* his death were necessary."

"How do you know that? Besides, what right did you have to decide *for* us?" Jakob's voice rose in anger.

Huddling with their mothers, the troll brothers flinched at the sound.

For a minute Jakob couldn't go on, remembering the head under the table, the familiar eyes staring sightlessly at him. His voice was strained, almost a whisper. "I didn't mean to kill anyone."

"Not again," Foss said, and this time he did yawn. But when Jakob's eyes flashed at him, he immediately apologized. Or as close to an apology as he could get. "You have killed no one, human child. Aenmarr killed his son. His wives killed Aenmarr."

Jakob frowned. "Technically . . ."

"I do not know this *technically*. Nor do I need to. But when you are home again, you will know better."

"Maybe. But you can't be sure."

"Nothing about the outside world is sure, human child. But in Trollholm there are things that are certain. For example, it is certain that trolls are mean, ugly, stupid, hungry . . ."

"And fossegrims?"

"There is only one."

"So you are it, our only way out."

The fox said nothing.

Jakob thought about this, leaning back in the big chair once again. "So, once we return you to your other shape, you can get us all out of here? Every human—princesses included?"

"Yes, child of man," Foss replied. "Yes, I can."

"Okay," Jakob said, and let his eyelids droop, shutting out the troll house as easily as the shutters kept out the sunlight. "It's a deal."

"A deal?" Foss asked.

Jakob smiled. "A pact," he explained before falling into a deep and much-needed sleep.

GALEN AND ERIK RETURNED, CARRYING a princess apiece who they set down next to the others. They were quarreling about which girl was heavier and their squabbling woke Jakob. He looked down at the girls as his brothers went back for more. There were already ten girls lying there, side by side.

He'd no idea how long he'd slept. Seconds? Minutes? Longer? He didn't dare let that happen again. After all, he'd promised Moira to keep watch. But his nap hadn't changed anything. The fox still lay head on paws, as before. The three troll wives were alive and breathing, their sons by their sides.

"What about them?" Jakob asked the fox, gesturing toward the enchanted girls, pretending he'd never nodded off.

"When I return to my true form," Foss answered, "I will lift the spell on them."

"How?"

"Magic." The fox refused to say more.

Jakob nodded, but noticed Selvi looking in his direction. She shook her head slightly, winked, then turned away. Jakob glanced back at Foss, but the fox's eyes were closed. He didn't seem to have noticed the troll wife's signal.

If it was a signal.

Jakob was just too tired to figure out what Selvi meant by the wink. *I'll just have to play it by ear.* Smiling at his own poor music joke, Jakob rested his eyelids again until Galen and Erik returned with the last princess, a tall, slim, handsome African American girl, with her crown perched on a head full of dreadlocks.

"Come on, sleepyhead," Galen called up to him. "We could

have used some help here. They may be princesses, but they aren't lightweights."

Jakob climbed down from the chair and helped them lay out the last girl, smoothing her dress down over her knees.

"When do you think Moira will be back?" Erik asked Jakob. But before Jakob could do more than shrug, Moira came bounding through the larder door, carrying the fiddle over her head.

"I'm here," she cried, her breath in short pants. Obviously she'd been running. She noticed all the girls and counted them quickly. Then she grinned. "Let's go home!"

Foss leapt to his feet, yipping with excitement. Botvi and Trigvi jumped up as well. Apparently, they weren't as hurt as they'd appeared. They crossed the room in two heavy troll steps, heavy enough to shake the floor. Botvi grabbed up Moira, and Trigvi plucked the fiddle from her grasp. It was done with such precision, they must have planned it in advance, though, for the life of him, Jakob couldn't have said when.

Moira squealed.

Erik cursed.

Galen yelled, "Ladies! What are you doing?"

"Stopping the Fossegrim," Selvi said from the floor.

Foss growled at the trolls, showing his teeth, and the troll wives flinched. But Trigvi and Botvi didn't drop their burdens.

"See!" screamed Foss in Jakob's mind. "This is what you get for trusting trolls."

Erik ran past the troll wives into the larder and came out

again carrying the two knives used to cut the brothers and Moira down earlier. The knives were half as big as he was. "I never trusted them," he said, tossing one of the knives to Galen who caught it awkwardly.

"Good child," Foss said. "Now, kill them!"

But Galen didn't move, for he, at least, had heard no orders.

"Wait!" Jakob shouted.

"Yeah," Moira said. "Wait. I don't need one of you idiots to stab me accidentally."

Galen froze, and Jakob threw himself in front of Erik, who looked ready to charge. "Hold on," he said softly, putting his hands on his brother's chest.

Trigvi held the fiddle by the neck in one hand, as if she were about to smash it against the wall. "Be going now, ill-omened creature. Be gone from our house."

Foss growled deep in his throat. The hackles on his neck bristled. "If the troll woman smashes my fiddle, none of you will ever leave this place."

Trigvi hauled her arm back and Jakob shouted, "Wait!" Turning to Selvi, he said, "Mama Selvi, make her wait, please."

Trigvi and Selvi exchanged glances. "Be saying your piece, Little Doom," Selvi said.

Jakob took a deep breath. "We need him, Mama Selvi. I don't trust him, either. But if we are to forge a new Compact—one where I teach your boys to play, and Moira teaches you ladies to sing—then you are going to have to trust me." Jakob swallowed and tried to stand up straighter, puff his chest out. "I am not the Fossegrim. I am not Aenmarr. I am

Jakob Griffson, musician. And I swear I will not deceive you."

For a moment, he was afraid that Selvi hadn't been convinced by his speech, for she was frowning. The lines on her forehead were like canyons and she sat as still as her stone husband. It was clear that trolls were not fast thinkers. But were they deep thinkers?

Finally Selvi nodded, her giant head moving slowly. Once to Jakob, and once to Trigvi.

"Be giving Little Doom the fiddle," she said.

Trigvi snapped her head around. "But . . ."

"Now!" Selvi snapped.

Trigvi placed the fiddle in Jakob's hands and then turned away.

It looked like no violin he'd ever seen. Intricate patterns were drawn on the body, and the neck was thick with mother-of-pearl and bone inlay. Strangely, it had more tuning pegs than playable strings, with half of the strings disappearing beneath the fingerboard.

Jakob looked at Foss. "How am I'm supposed to play this? I'm a guitarist not . . ."

Foss interrupted. "With the girl." He looked up at Botvi who was still holding Moira by the arm.

"The girl is going to have a bit of trouble doing anything," Moira said, "if I'm not set down!"

"Mama Selvi?" Jakob begged.

Selvi nodded to Botvi, her great head moving slowly up and down like a balanced stone. Just as slowly, Botvi let Moira down to the floor.

"All right," Selvi said, "now we be hearing you play."

· 25 ·

Moira

Moira felt awkward. She had her arms wrapped around Jakob, left hand on his elbow, right holding a bow. Jakob had the fiddle tucked under his chin, the neck balanced on his left thumb.

Foss pranced around them. "Good, good. Pull your elbow up a little, human girl. Good."

"Let's get on with it, Foss," Moira said.

"We will begin when you are ready. And I will say when you are ready." Foss looked at her critically. "I would rather not have you two miss a note and turn me into a cuttlefish."

"A what?" Jakob asked.

"A cousin of an octopus," Moira said. "Don't you know anything?"

Foss sighed. "All right, we will try a simple song."

"But we still don't know how to play this thing," Moira

said. "Is it a fiddle or a harp? A sitar or a guitar? Techniques differ, you know. Pluck, strum, bow . . ."

"You are musicians," the fox shot back.

"Well, *I* am." Moira frowned at the back of Jakob's head. "*He's* a pop star."

"Hey!" Jakob said.

"Sorry, Jakob," she said, "but it's true. You're not a *real* musician."

"And you are? Because you play *classical*?"

The tone of his voice set her teeth on edge. She'd dealt with this kind of thing before. "Look, every teenager who strums a guitar thinks he's the next . . ." She paused, realizing she didn't know who teenage guitarists would want to be. "Andrés Segovia," she finished lamely.

"Andrés who?"

"See!" Moira turned to Foss. "One of the greatest guitarists of all time, and he doesn't even know the name." Sneering at Jakob, she said, "Because Andrés Segovia was a *classical* guitarist."

Jakob's face burned bright red. He opened his mouth to retort but Foss interrupted, barking his annoyance at them.

"You both know what music is, and how to make it." He sighed again. "Now pay attention."

"What are they talking about?" Galen said to Erik. "And who are they talking to?"

"Haven't got it yet, big brother?" Erik paused. "The fox speaks in their heads." He smiled. "And mine."

"I don't hear anything."

"He only speaks to real musicians," Moira snapped.

Galen glowered. "And what do you call me?"

"Front man," Erik said.

Foss ignored the exchange as he circled around them. When he spoke again, it was only to Moira and Jakob. "The fiddle is in the *huldastilt* tuning. Most *hardanger* fiddles would be useless after playing a song in this tuning. But the Fossegrim's fiddle is an exceptional instrument. The body is of wood cut from *Yggdrasil,* the world tree. Bones of the great worm, Fafnir, line its fingerboard. The playing strings are wound from the guts of the cats that pulled Frigga's carriage; the understrings forged from the same metal as Sigmund's sword."

"Yada, yada, yada," Jakob said. "Get on with it."

But Moira had dealt with composers and conductors easily as arrogant as Foss. The only thing one could do was wait patiently until they grew tired of the sound of their own voices. Eventually, they'd want to hear some music.

"Little Doom, you will guide the melody with your nimble left hand."

"While I flail madly away with the bow?" Moira said. This time she couldn't help herself. Standing with her arms around Jakob was embarrassing if they weren't actually playing music.

Jakob twisted to look at her and shook his head.

Shut up Moira, she told herself.

Foss didn't react to her sarcasm. Instead he said, "You have had some training in bowed instruments. I can see it in your fingers."

Moira gasped. How had he known? She hadn't actually played a bowed instrument since elementary school where she'd taken two years of Suzuki lessons on a quarter-size violin.

Ignoring her reverie, the fox continued his instructions. "Do not rely on the bow overmuch. The *hardanger* is different from anything you have played before. And the Fosse-grim *hardanger* even more so." He finally stopped circling and stood before them. "I will put the song in your mind. You have only to let it out through your fingers."

Moira's eyes widened. That's exactly how she felt at times, reading a new piece, or playing an old familiar one—as if the songs filled her to bursting, and shot out of her fingers on to the strings.

"Ah," said Foss, "you begin to understand."

Moira nodded.

"Then let us play. This is 'Fille Vern,' a simple dance tune." He bared his teeth. "I am sure your trolls will enjoy it."

Just like that, she and Jakob began playing. And as Foss had said, there was a song in their minds, and now they were releasing it onto the fiddle.

Moira's right hand with the bow sawed back and forth in two-four time. Jakob's fingers moved confidently over the strings. The rhythm was contagious, and Moira began tapping her foot in time. When she found she had some small control over her right arm, she leaned into it on the nearly atonal bridge, adding some accents that were all her own.

Foss raised an eyebrow at her.

Grinning her defiance at him, she thought: *You may call the tune, but we still play it our way.*

Then Jakob played a trill that Moira was certain Foss

hadn't put in their minds, and the fox's other eyebrow went up, too.

Moira laughed out loud then, laughed for the sheer joy of playing, for the pure sound of music and the feeling it gave her. And Jakob laughed with her, their limbs moving in concert, the music flowing as if they were one person.

The song ended too soon. Staring at the back of Jakob's head, Moira thought, *Maybe I judged him too quickly.* And when he twisted back again to look at her, she shot him a smile so bright it made his cheeks blossom red. *Sorry,* she thought. But she didn't say it out loud.

Sitting on his haunches, Foss stared at them. The seconds stretched into minutes and the fox's eyes got darker and his nose twitched. Suddenly he reminded Moira of the Maestro who often waited like that, stretching the agony out, before finally commenting on the section just played.

"Well," he said finally, "it seems that the two of you are more ready than I had imagined."

Moira was pleased and she felt Jakob's shoulders relax.

Standing, Foss balanced himself awkwardly on his hind feet. "Let us begin again."

Moira smiled to herself. That was just what Maestro liked to say: *Let us begin again.*

This time the song that crept into her mind seemed much more subtle and complex than the dance number they'd just played. Its time signature was some bizarre compound of prime numbers. The melody was haunting and insistent, and the tones that rang from the fiddle's understrings accented it in odd and unfamiliar ways.

She watched Foss carefully as they played, as if he were a

conductor. And in two ways he *was,* she realized, not only leading them in the music but also soon he'd be conducting them home.

But then she noticed something truly odd. Unlike a human orchestra conductor who beats out the time, who cues the musicians in, who works for the good of the music, the fox was paying absolutely no attention to them. Instead, he was focused on himself. As the music swelled, he began to change. His red hair disappeared, receding like a tide into his hide. His nose and ears shrank. His back legs grew bigger, longer, developed knees, flexible ankles. When his paws turned into hands, he let out a gasp and flexed his fingers reverently. Only his eyes remained the same, unreadable black orbs. The changes came slowly at first, then faster and faster as the tune continued.

As her bow and Jakob's fingers danced over the fiddle and its strings, strange scenes leaped into Moira's head: a long wooden boat crashing into heavy dark seas, rows of burly men heaving at the oars; a lone figure capering around a bonfire, fiddle in hand; a waterfall with a cave behind it. She recognized the last spot. It was the cave Foss lived in, but there was no worn path leading to it, only a scruff of grass. The trees surrounding the river, another painted backdrop, barely saplings.

Suddenly, Moira realized she was seeing through Foss's eyes. Or at least, through his memories. Somehow, to give him back his old form, they were playing his entire history.

Jakob turned his head and stared wide-eyed back at her. Moira guessed he'd experienced the same burst of history. She tried to speak aloud to him but she found she couldn't. *Ride it out,* she thought.

Jakob looked away.

Then she saw that Foss's change was nearly complete. Though small pieces of red fur still stood out on his pale skin—a beard, a mustache, patches at his wrist—they were fading fast. He looked almost like a normal person, Normal, except for those eyes.

Moira expected the song to end when the transformation ended. But she and Jakob kept playing, even as Foss stood, now an alarmingly naked young man of maybe twenty, with long teeth and rust-red hair.

Why? Moira thought before answering her own question: *Because we're not done.*

With a nod from Foss the conductor, the tune's tempo doubled, and Moira suddenly felt something pouring out of her. *Energy, life force, something.* Whatever it was, she didn't like that it was leaving her—and apparently entering Foss. She looked up into his dark eyes and he smiled the same toothy grin he had when he'd been a fox.

Oh no, she thought, horrified. *He's tricked us! He never once intended to let us go.*

As they fiddled, their tune more frantic than before, the scenes from Foss' early life rushed through Moira's brain. She saw him turning from fox to man and back again. Watched a young tree-tall Aenmarr knock the fiddle from Foss's grip mid-transformation. Saw Foss swearing eternal revenge on the troll and all his kind as Aenmarr capered away, laughing uproariously.

"Yes," Foss said, able to speak aloud for now he once again had a human mouth and human vocal chords. "You will never leave this place. And I am truly sorry. You are both very talented musicians."

Hearing this, Erik lunged at the fox.

With a sweep of his arm, Foss hurled a wave of sound that caught Erik in the chest, sending him flying into the wall. His head hit with a *thud* and he crumpled to the ground.

Foss spoke louder now for the fiddle was practically screaming in its quest for higher notes. "I could have taught you music such as you have never heard. Music to sway the minds of kings and change the hearts of queens. Music to command armies and set foes to flight. Music to make gray-beards dance and the lame to walk."

He'd hardly finished, when Galen jumped at him, aiming a sloppy overhand blow for his chin. Foss shouted a single syllable. It seemed to stop Galen in his tracks and he looked at his chest for a moment, then collapsed.

"Blood and music flow much the same," Foss said. "And I need a fair amount of both to complete my change."

The troll women stirred and Foss simply growled at them. Selvi shot Moira a look full of resignation and just a touch of *I told you so,* before clutching her boy to her bosom and subsiding with the other two wives.

No! Moira thought. *We have to stop him.* I *have to stop him.*

She tried to move independently, tried to change the song as she had with the dance tune. Tried to change keys, meter, time signature. Anything. But the song had her fully in its grip, and she couldn't substitute a single note or phrase. She looked at Jakob, saw him gritting his teeth and grimacing at his left hand as if he were trying the same thing.

And having no more luck than I.

"Child of man," Foss said. Then grinned. "And woman. It will all be over in moments. And I do thank you for all your help." He bowed low, like a courtier in an ancient court. "I quite literally could not have done it without you."

Moira raged and screamed internally, all the while, her right arm bowing the notes that would soon bring about the end of her life and those around her.

Notes! She kept her face clear of her excitement. *That's it!* She'd suddenly remembered how annoyed Foss had been when she'd whistled off key. As if the merest nonmusical sound didn't just bother him. It caused him actual discomfort.

She abandoned her attempt to control her arm. In fact, she gave it even more fully to the Fossegrim, thinking: *Let him have it.*

Relaxing, she threw herself into the music completely. Well, almost completely. She let Foss have her arms, her legs, her body. Let him have everything but one thing. And she concentrated on that thing, concentrated harder than she ever had over a difficult piece of music, or a tricky fingering on the harp. Harder than she ever had for any test or practice or performance. Concentrated every part of her being solely on her own mouth.

Then with one massive effort, she managed to croak out one word.

"Notes."

Foss arched an eyebrow. "Notes? I do not understand you, human child." He shrugged. "Not that it will matter."

Moira could feel herself fading, disappearing even as she kept bowing. As for Jakob, she could hear his breath rattling in his chest. But his fingers still flew over the guts and bone of the fiddle's neck.

Foss stretched his new arms, hunched his sinewy shoulders. "It feels good to wear my true skin once more."

Moira ignored him. Ignored the pain in her chest and her arms, and the fading, sinking feeling. She ignored everything but the need to send that one word across the room. Across to the troll boys nestled in their mother's arms.

"Notes," she rasped.

Buri looked up at her. She tried to encourage him, make him understand. But that effort made her concentration lapse, and she lost control of her mouth. She knew she wouldn't have the strength to try again.

I never even got to play the new Berlin piece. Even as she had the thought, she realized what a stupid thing it was to regret. What about all the other things she'd never get to do? *I'll never graduate, never move to New York and join a big symphony, never get married, never . . .* She would have sobbed if she'd had control of her tear ducts.

Just then Jakob—who must have understood her—spoke up. He'd saved up his energy for three whole words. "Arri. Buri. Notes!"

The troll boys looked up at him, then back at their mothers.

"Sing!" Selvi encouraged them.

"Be singing your notes," Trigvi added.

"I do not be knowing why, boys," Botvi said, "but sing!"

And grinning widely, Arri and Buri burst into glorious

song, their astonishing lack of pitch topped only by their truly horrific timbre. It was awful and terrific at the same time.

Foss flinched and Moira felt a rip in the web of music that held her.

The fox shook a fist at the trolls and Arri went flying, but the spell missed Buri, and he sang louder to make up for his fallen brother.

That moment gave Moira an opening. She managed to twitch her bow arm, skipping the note that should have been there.

Jakob, too, was loosed for that moment, and he played an octave and two, where a fifth was called for. It was truly awful.

Screaming, Foss glared at them, but the three troll women suddenly lent their horrendous screeching to the cacophony and Foss dropped to one knee as if punched in the stomach.

"Oh, by Frigg and Freya," he groaned. "That is horrible."

And it is, Moira thought. *Horrible and wonderful.*

Arri stood, shook himself off, and began singing "Hang down, Drool, hang down Drool," over and over at the top of his lungs.

The troll women chanted the "Little Doom Song," while young Buri just howled one long note until he collapsed unconscious, having forgotten to take a breath.

Blood ran out of Foss' ears and he clamped his hands over them to staunch the flow. Then standing, he shuffled backward toward the larder. On the way he slipped on the water that Moira had wrung from the cloths and this time went down on both knees. When he tried to stand again, all the energy he had stolen from Moira and Jakob rushed out of him like a river in spate, and flowed back into them. He only made it to one hairy knee before Galen and Erik scraped themselves off the floor and knocked him over with a double-flying tackle.

Then the troll women jumped on him as well, and the sound that he made as he went down under them was something like a tire deflating.

In seconds it was over. Foss was gagged and hog-tied with two troll boys sitting on him for good measure. He was not fully human but not fully fox, either, just somewhere in between.

"Hey, girl—what's going on?"

Moira looked over in surprise. Helena was sitting up and rubbing her eyes. Her crown had fallen off and her dreads were all askew. "Moira?" she asked tremulously. "Where in God's green world are we?"

The Dairy Princesses had begun to awaken.

Jakob

It was chaos. Eleven startled girls, muzzy and fuzzy from days of sleep, all talking at once; Moira trying to raise her voice above them to explain; Trigvi and Botvi bustling about preparing a meal for their many guests; and the troll boys busy competing with Jakob's brothers, each trying to outdo the other in their efforts to impress the beautiful girls.

If the princesses noticed anything strange about their green-skinned hosts, they were too polite to say. Or too befuddled with sleep and enchantment.

Jakob watched it all from the wall where he sat next to Selvi. She cradled her broken arm in her lap and had the other curled protectively around Little Doom.

"Mama Selvi," Jakob said. "I don't think we can forge a new Compact."

"Why not?" Selvi boomed in her quietest voice. "Be you not trusting me?"

"I *do* trust you." Jakob patted the big green hand that rested on his shoulder. "But without Foss's help, we'll never get back to our own world. I'll still teach your boys to play, but we certainly can't bring you any butter."

Selvi looked down at him, a perplexed look on her face. "Why be you needing the Fossegrim? You already be having his fiddle."

Jakob sighed. "Yes, but we don't really know how to play it. That was all Foss's doing."

Selvi chuckled. It was like the boom of a waterfall. "Silly Little Doom. You be not needing to play it. The fiddle be of both worlds. Whoever holds it can be passing through at will. Foss the fox could be going only to the middle of the bridge, no farther because he not be having the fiddle to hand. As for Aenmarr, he be not knowing the fiddle's power. Really, troll men be not very smart." She grinned and winked at him.

Jakob sat up straight. "Really?"

"Really," Selvi answered.

"Then why did you not take the fiddle and go?"

She was silent for a long time. *Deep thinking*, he supposed. "Be looking at me, Little Doom," she said at last. "Be really looking at me. How could I be making my way, how could my son, in the world of men? They would be knowing me for what I am and be killing me and mine. As long ago, so it be now."

He nodded. "There are many humans who would not understand," he said. "Who would hate you. But some . . ."

She smiled at him and shifted beside him. It was like a mountain moving. "Then we be welcoming such 'somes' if they be liking to visit us here."

But he knew, as she knew, that no one but he and Moira and possibly his brothers would ever come across the bridge into Trollholm. It could be a quiet place, out of the world, when things got too hard for them. But who else could they trust with the secret? He turned and looked deeply into her eyes.

She looked back. "Now, Little Doom, let us be making our new Compact out of trust, not fear. Out of love, not hate."

Jakob beamed. "I'll write a song about it."

"And then be teaching it to us?" Selvi asked.

Jakob nodded enthusiastically. "And then be teaching it to all of you."

He stood and clapped his hands together till he had everyone's attention, not easy above that hubbub. But at last he managed it. This time even his brothers listened.

"Hey," he said. "We be going home."

COMPACT
I give to you,
A promise made,
From fate to fate
The game is played.
The music slides on
Note by note,
We look for love,
We live on hope.

The bridge across
The waters wide
Cannot hold back
The surging tide.
Beneath the falls
We sit and wait
To see what love
Transforms to hate.

And I will hold out friendship's hand,
Heart to heart and land to land.

The larder's full,
The pot is boiled,
The plan is laid,
The plot is foiled,
The fire's set,
The flames are high,
The flag's unfurled
Against the sky.

The war is joined,
The bullet milled,
The wound is open,
Blood is spilled.
And hate is answered
Fast by hate,

The peaceful word
Is spoke too late.

Still I will hold out friendship's hand,
Heart to heart and land to land.
Still I will hold out friendship's hand,
Across the bridge, from land to land.

—Words and music by
Jakob and Erik Griffson
and Moira Darr,
from *Troll Bridge*

Radio WMSP: 10:00 A.M.

"*So there's been a huge break in the Dairy Princess case, Jim?*"

"*Yes, Katie—everyone is safe. Everyone except Mr. Sjogren the photographer who gave his life for the girls. There will be a memorial service for him Sunday here in Vanderby and next week in the Twin Cities.*"

"*A hero, Jim?*"

"*A real hero, according to Moira Darr, the harp prodigy who is the only one of the princesses who actually remembers anything of what happened on the fateful day they were kidnapped by the madman, Grimma Foss.*"

"*Are the kids okay, Jim?*"

"*You betcha. Except for a few bumps and lumps. The youngest Griffson boy, Jakob, has some burns, plus a hairline fracture of his right tibia. The middle boy, Erik, has quite a shiner. The oldest, Galen, has marks around his wrists and ankles where he was tied, upside down by his own account, though he's*" been very funny and charming about the whole thing. The girls—except for Moira who'd gotten away early—were treated rather better until the end. Administered some kind of knockout drug. The police chief says the doctors are still trying to figure that one out."

"Still, they must have been frightened."

"Yah, I can't even begin to imagine it, Katie. Four days under the thumb of that madman. The Dairy Princess Association has committed to hiring bodyguards for their contestants. It's a different world we live in now."

"How did they finally escape, Jim?"

"Somehow they got loose of their bonds, overwhelmed Foss, tied him up, and brought him back over the bridge. There he went stark raving mad. Evidently he was planning to 'marry' the girls and kill the boys."

"He must have been stark raving mad all along, Jim."

"I agree, Katie. Jakob Griffson told us that Foss said he was a musician down on his luck, which was how he managed to get the boys into his clutches. Seems they're suckers for such a story."

"Bet they won't be such suckers anymore, Jim."

"Yah, I imagine not. Now I did some interviews I'd like you to hear, the first with young Moira."

<click>

"Are you relieved to be free, Moira?"

"I'm relieved we're all free, Mr. Johnson."

"Of course you are. Now, according to the boys, you were quite the heroine."

"I think I was just lucky, Mr. Johnson."

"Lucky?"

"Lucky to have friends like Jakob Griffson."

<click>

"Well, Jim, that certainly is a composed young woman. Must be all that stage training. Hmmm, do you suppose there's something going on between . . ."

"He's fifteen and a half, Katie, and she's sixteen going on thirty-five. But here's what Jakob had to say."

<click>

"We'd never have escaped that madman without Moira's help. For a classical musician, she's quite something."

<click>

"And the other brothers, Jim?"

"They said almost the same thing."

"Should that be the last word on the story then?"

"No, Katie, I think that should belong to Mr. Foss."

<click>

"BLAME IT ON THE TROLLS! AENMARR DID IT. AND NOW HE'S A ROCK. ROCK AND TROLL. AIEEEEEE."

<click>

"Who is Aenmarr, Jim? An accomplice?"

"A troll, or so Foss says."

"You mean like . . . I'm a troll, fol-de-rol, nine feet tall and nine feet wide, mean and green and hungry, Jim?"

"[Laughs.] The police have been all over the area and they've found no indication of anyone else involved. The kids swear it was Foss who was behind their disappearance. Foss and no one else. And they have absolutely no reason to lie about it."

"Thanks, Jim. And now to Bob with the sports. How about those Timberwolves, Bob?"

∾ Songs from Troll Bridge ∾

BUTTER GIRLS

Twelve dairy princesses, where did they go?
Twelve dairy princesses, I'd really like to know.

The Devil snatched them from thin air
So they couldn't make it to the fair
And now's he's gone and taken them below.

And he was singing:
What's better than a butter girl?
Badder than my better girl.
Best when I'm not buttered up as well.
What's better than a butter girl?
Badder than my better girl.
Best that I just take them all to Hell.

Twelve dairy princesses sleeping in a box,
Pretty plastic tiaras upon their curly locks.
Grim the groom who grabbed them up
And made them drink the poisoned cup,
And now he's got them caught behind cold locks.

And he was singing:
What's better than a butter girl?
Badder than my better girl.
Best when I'm not buttered up as well.

What's better than a butter girl?
Badder than my better girl.
Best that I just take them all to Hell.

TELLER, TELLER

Teller, teller, tell me a tale,
Of love and fear and duty,
I want to die in the arms of love,
I want to die for beauty.
For beauty is the only truth,
And death the only lie,
I want to sing a final tale,
And love before I die.

So tell me quick,
If I've been heard,
Else, maim with a phrase,
Kill with a word.

Princess, princess, give me a kiss,
A kiss of love, of pleasure,
I want to lie in the arms of love,
I want to sing of treasure.
For passion is the only truth,
And death the only lie,
I want to know your lips on mine,
And love before I die.

So tell me quick,
If I've been heard,
Else, maim with a phrase,
Kill with a word.

HUNG UP FOR DINNER

Long pig, sweet meat,
Strong swig, fleet treat,
I don't want to be hung up.
For dinner.

Short tale, long death,
Quart ale, wrong breath,
I don't want to be hung up.
For dinner.

Give me a choice of meat or soy,
Give me a choice of girl or boy,
Give me a choice or give me chance,
A great big meal or a real romance.

Slow boil, quick take,
Low oil, thick steak,
I don't want to be hung up.
For dinner.

Hot ice, cold drink,
Caught twice, old stink,

I don't want to be hung up.
Over dinner.

DOOM
Doom, Doom, Doom
Come back.
In my wee room
I'll hack and whack.

I'll cleft your skull,
And split your skin,
From crotch to jowl,
From toes to chin.

And then I'll make
A tasty stew,
And in I'll take
The rest of you.

Doom, Doom, Doom,
Doom, Doom, Doom.

Doom, Doom, Doom
I'm back.
My fiery room
Goes crackle and crack.

I'll tell you true
And I'll not lie,

I'll give to you
A chance to fly.

And then we'll make
Another pact
Or else I'll take
Your living back.

Doom, Doom, Doom,
Doom, Doom, Doom.

Doom, Doom, Doom
I'm back.
My fiery room
Goes crackle and crack.

The Dairy Queen,
Who wears the crown,
Can be real mean
And wear you down,

So make a deal
Another pact
Or you will feel
Your sons hijacked.

Doom, Doom, Doom,
Doom, Doom, Doom.

PRINCE CHARMING COMES

The goose flies past the setting sun,
Plums roasting in her breast,
Sleeping Beauty lays her head down,
A hundred years to rest.
And fee-fi-fo the giant fums,
And to my dark Prince Charming comes
A-ride, ride, riding.
Into my night of darkness
My own Prince Charming comes.

The witch is popped into the oven,
Rising into cake,
The swan queen glides her downy form,
To the enchanted lake.
And rum-pum-pum the drummer drums,
As into darkness my prince comes
A-ride, ride, riding.
Into my night of darkness
My own Prince Charming comes.

It's half past twelve and once again
The shoe of glass is gone,
And magic is as magic was,
And vanished with the dawn.
For Pooh has hummed his final hum,
The giant finished off his fums,
They've drawn their final breath,
For into darkness my prince comes
A-ride, ride, riding.

For into darkness my prince comes,
On his bony horse called Death.

COMPACT
I give to you,
A promise made,
From fate to fate
The game is played.
The music slides on
Note by note,
We look for love,
We live on hope.

The bridge across
The waters wide
Cannot hold back
The surging tide.
Beneath the falls
We sit and wait
To see what love
Transforms to hate.

And I will hold out friendship's hand,
Heart to heart and land to land.

The larder's full,
The pot is boiled,
The plan is laid,
The plot is foiled,

The fire's set,
The flames are high,
The flag's unfurled
Against the sky.

The war is joined,
The bullet milled,
The wound is open,
Blood is spilled.
And hate is answered
Fast by hate,
The peaceful word
Is spoke too late.

Still I will hold out friendship's hand,
Heart to heart and land to land.
Still I will hold out friendship's hand,
Across the bridge, from land to land.